Just A Drop in the Cup

Diane Arrelle

JERSEY PINES INK

This is a work of fiction. Names, characters, businesses, places, events, locales and incidents are either the products of the authors' imagination or used in a fictitious manner. Any resemblance to actual persons, living or dead, or actual events is purely coincidental.

All rights reserved, including the right to reproduce this book or portions thereof in any form whatsoever.

The publisher is not responsible for websites or their content that are not owned by the publisher

Interior Design— River Cove Productions
Cover art — Dar Albert, Wicked Smart Designs
Copyright © 2021 Jersey Pines Ink
ISBN 978-1-948899-10-9

This book is dedicated to Tom for all his love and support in the face of that most difficult of adversities: marriage. It is also dedicated to my children, Kat and Stephen, who have always been my sources of inspiration, frustration and adoration. I love you all.

Welcome to
JUST A DROP IN THE CUP

Forty-two drabbles, micro stories, flash fiction stories and slightly longer stories mixed into a robust brew consisting of fantasy, science fiction and suspense. They are steeped in horror and humor with no bitter aftertaste . . . well, with just a hint of bitterness and a lot of full flavored irony.

This book was originally published in 2007 by Darker Intensions Press, a company I am proud to have had publish my book. It was put together in 2005, and in the fifteen years since it was originally conceived, some of the stories did not age well due to changes in society and technology while others are currently published in other anthologies and ezines.

Now is the perfect time to rerelease this book, keeping nineteen of the original stories. I have also included eight new previously unpublished stories and fifteen more stories new to this book.

I hope you enjoy rereading your favorites and equally enjoy reading all the new stories in *Just A Drop In The Cup*.

DIANE ARRELLE

TABLE OF CONTENTS

Bad Luck Kitty	1
Long Ago, Far Away, Never Forgotten	6
Like Candles On A Cake, Make A Wish And Blow	10
The Soul Suckers	11
As Different As An Arm And A Leg	15
~~Paulie's~~ Harvey's Mom	19
Roses And Ivy	22
The Way We Were	26
Darn Them	27
Dig It	33
Just A Drop In The Cup	37
That Holiday Newsletter	41
A Small Brown Planet To Call Home	47
So Sorry . . . But . . .	48
Someday My Knight Will Come	52
Hungering For Anybody	59
Critic's Revenge	62
Grainy Nightmares	63
The Feast Of Stephen	67
A Walk In The Forest	73
Reflective Wishes	74
Slight Of Hand	78

Sense Of Self	79
The Oldest Man In The World	81
The Smart Phone	82
We Are Brady	88
C.O.D.D	91
Burning Away the Tears, Burning Away the Years	97
Debbie Does Deuce	98
The Sweetest Good-Bye	102
Badgers For Christmas	106
One Man's Trash	108
Bagging It	111
Do The Right Thing	115
Notches	119
Sleep Not	123
Not A Remote Chance	124
Filling The Hollow	128
Gingersnap Christmas	130
Not The Remotest Hope For Adam And Eve	134
To The Farm	135
A Small Misunderstanding	140

I love to walk a few miles every day, but sometimes barking dogs behind electric fences make me wonder if the shock is strong enough to keep them on their side and then I wonder, what if it isn't?

BAD LUCK KITTY

I guess you could say I was having a not-so-good day when the dog charged me. Up until I heard that snarling beast, it hadn't been a really bad day, just a typical spring day. You know, Sonny woke up with a hangover, told me how sorry he was about last night, then smacked me again for good measure. He said he was sorry . . . sorry he'd ever married me, sorry he'd ever knocked me up, sorry I was still around to remind him that all his hard earned money was wasted on me and Beth. He was sorry that I'd survived all the beatings, accidents, broken bones, and childbirth.

The only saving grace in my life was that Sonny was only a cheap, mean, nasty son of a bitch and not a homicidal one. At least not yet.

Anyway, I was taking a walk in the slightly chilly March air, nursing my bruised cheek and trying to figure out where Sonny hid the money so that Beth and I could take it and run away. All of a sudden I looked up and saw a black cat with a crooked tail cross my path. "That's just great!" I muttered, then shuddered. "Just what I need, some bad luck!"

As if in answer, I heard barking, and it was growing nearer. Not the nice kind of barking, but that growling, snarling kind. Then a monstrous dog crashed through the hedge on my left and charged at me. I froze. I read somewhere that you should never run, and I now knew why. That's because your legs are suddenly made of jelly, and if you try to run you'll only fall and make it easier for the dog to rip out your throat.

So I stood, frozen and waited to die, but the dog suddenly jerked to a stop. I could see it was part pit bull, part mastiff, and a big part Swamp Thing. With fangs bared and slobber hanging in long, dirty strings of drool, the dog stared off to my right and suddenly took off past me.

To say I was surprised was an understatement! I watched the charging hellhound and saw him running down that black cat. *Poor kitty,* I thought and felt a surge of relief as the cat headed for a tree. He was up it in a second, leaving the dog running in circles around it, yammering like crazy.

"Thanks kitty, seems you have the bad luck now," I whispered, then slowly walked away, leaving the two animals to work out their problems. I felt bad for the cat, but he was safe in the tree and maybe the dog would just run circles around the tree until he melted into a pool of butter.

Back home, I noticed Sonny's motorcycle was gone so I tiptoed into the garage and looked for the hiding place. Sonny didn't like banks; he just hid our money to be safe. Only it wasn't really our money, it was mine. It was my insurance settlement for the roof after that tornado. The house was still in my name. It belonged to my parents before they died. But Sonny, he took the money and fixed the roof himself. I know he stole supplies from the roofing company he'd been fired from. And from the way the back room leaked, I know why they canned him.

Then there's the money from the accident. Sonny had been mad because he was out of scotch. He yelled at me to get into the car. Going to the liquor store, he deliberately drove crazy to scare me, weaving from one side of the road to the other. Suddenly, another car was coming straight for us! Sonny swerved to get out of the way and the other driver did the same. It was a head-on collision. The other driver died and we were on the correct side of the road. Sonny sued the dead man's estate for all my pain and suffering. Sometimes I wonder if he did it to kill me. Too bad I never saw any of that money either.

I heard a sound and stiffened. I didn't want Sonny to find me, so I turned and went back outside. There was that black cat again. Strutting in front of me, acting like he forgave me for abandoning him after he saved my bacon. He strolled over and wove his way between my legs back and forth, and I could hear him purring like Sonny's bike on idle.

Glancing around to make sure Sonny was out wherever it was he liked to disappear, I stooped and picked the cat up. He fit perfectly in my arms and, still purring, he affectionately butted my chin with his head. I scratched him behind his ears and smiled. Few things make me smile anymore. Seeing my little girl laugh could always make me smile, but Beth hardly laughed now. She just kind of skulked around the house, trying to act invisible whenever her daddy graced us with his presence.

"Poor kitty cat," I said burying my face in the cat's soft, dark fur. "You're just a bad luck kitty. If Sonny sees you, you won't have enough lives to survive. He's one superstitious man!" I shuddered and remembered how he had broken a mirror and given me seven years of bad luck. Sonny never walked under a ladder or opened an umbrella in the house. Man, if he saw this black cat it could scare him to death. Thinking that thought, I realized I'd finally found another thing that could make me smile.

I put the cat down and went inside to fill a bowl with milk. I'd make sure to feed him far away from the house so Sonny wouldn't find him and kill him. I finally had a friend, and I wasn't about to lose him to the maniac I'd unfortunately married.

I took the bowl out and frowned. My new friend was nowhere to be seen. Leaving the back door ajar, I wandered the neighborhood calling, "Here kitty, here cat."

I felt like crying when I realized he had split. *Just like a man*, I thought with a bitter laugh. *Love 'em and leave 'em.* Then I really laughed; laughed so hard I started to cry. If only Sonny had followed that old adage, I'd be a happy woman today. Someday I'm going to find that money, then it's goodbye bastard.

I returned home, went in the slightly opened door and felt panic clawing at my throat. This day was just getting worse and worse. The cat had gotten inside and walked in the fireplace then on the carpet. I saw the trail of dark gray pawprints and wanted to scream. How was I going to clean this up before Sonny returned? He'd see the prints and beat me for sure. Then I noticed the prints led from the fireplace to a pile of logs on the floor. Sonny warned me to leave them alone when I cleaned. "You never know when I'm going to want to make a fire," he said. "So don't mess with my wood unless you want to cut down a tree and lug it in here yourself."

I always figured that the firewood in the corner was just another of Sonny's quirks. He had a lot of quirks. I once moved them looking for the money, but he saw they'd been rearranged and hit me. I never touched them again. But now the cat was sitting on one log with his tail twitching. "Rouwull," the cat growled and pawed at the side of the wood.

I walked over to him, following his pawprints, and stared at the log. It looked normal enough, but then the cat pawed it a little harder and it rolled off the pile.

How could a cat swat a heavy log off the woodpile, I wondered, and stooped to pick it up. It was light, like it had been hollowed out. I took it outside and studied it. One end was false like a plug in a bottle. I pried it opened. It was full of money! Not all the money, but a good two grand.

"Well kitty," I said, picking up the cat. "You seem to be my hero. Somehow, I'm going to have to figure out a way to keep you. If only you could show me where the rest of the money is hidden."

"Meow," the cat exclaimed and started to purr. I gave him a hug, and to my surprise he leapt from my arms and ran out the still opened back door.

I dashed out after him, yelling, "Come back!" But he was history.

Annoyed and hurt, I picked up the log and put it back together enough so that Sonny wouldn't realize it was tampered with. I stuck it back on the pile. It looked fine to me. Then I sat in the kitchen and counted my money. Nineteen hundred dollars; yep, it was the roof money. What I needed to find was the insurance settlement. That was the real cash.

I glanced at the clock and realized the carpet was still soiled with cat prints. I'd been so preoccupied with the money I'd forgotten to vacuum. Beth would be home soon and I went out to meet the bus, hoping Sonny'd stay out another hour and give me time to clean up.

To my surprise, a patrol car was pulling into my driveway. What trouble did Sonny get into this time, I wondered with a huge, resigned sigh. Maybe if he needed to be bailed out he'd tell me where he'd hidden the rest of the money. Wouldn't that be great!

Instead, two officers came up to me and gently led me back inside. Then they broke the news. Sonny'd had an accident while apparently on his way home. He'd been drinking and . . . and according to witnesses had swerved off the road to avoid hitting a black cat. He'd died instantly.

The officers stood waiting for my response, the hysterics. I sat stunned. Finally, I managed to speak. "Oh my God, did the cat have a crooked tail? He didn't hit it, did he?"

That night after the cops left and the arrangements for the cremation were made, I went outside to put out another dish of milk and a plate of tuna. I wasn't disappointed. My cat was sitting on the back stoop, waiting. He ran over to his well-earned dinner and gobbled it up, then sat at the door as if waiting to be let in. I opened it and he entered like the new king of the house. Maybe he'll help me find the rest of my money, but there was no rush anymore. Sonny had been insured.

"Thank you, kitty," I told him and picked him up. "I guess it would be tacky to call you Lucky," I added, hugging my cat.

But I did anyway.

Alien abduction? What if they are just looking for a good conversation?

LONG AGO, FAR AWAY, NEVER FORGOTTEN

It was long ago and it was far away and it had never been forgotten. The words echoed in Janine's head. Over and over. And she missed him.

It had started simply enough. Just a late-night drive to escape her husband and her children for an hour. The noise, the fighting, the *he did it, no she did it first* broken record that played every night as Gerald sat in front of the television watching some sports event. She'd learned too late that it didn't matter what sport: baseball, football, soccer, hockey, whatever it was, he'd plant himself in front of the TV and become instantly mesmerized. Janine was sure he'd react the same way to naked mud wrestling as to a basketball game. The television was his escape from the daily stress and hers was long, quiet drives.

She remembered taking the road that had cornfields on both sides, blackness as far as she could see in every direction. Not another car in sight. Janine floored it and zoomed down the straight away, feeling free and happy. "I could go on like this and never go back," she yelled, and imagined Gerald suddenly having to deal with three bickering kids.

She smiled and went faster. Faster than she ever drove before. Suddenly she was blinded by a purple light and heard a loud *pop* next to her. Screaming, she jerked the wheel, and the car careened out of control, plowing into the field off to her right.

Pain, she was in so much pain. She could see blood splattered like black streaks in the dim dashboard light. She wondered if she was dying or was already dead.

"I'm sorry," the male voice said, "I startled you."

A voice? Where the hell did a voice come from? "Can't you see I'm dying?" Janine said with a weak moan. "What just happened?"

"Hmmmm, yes, I see. You are dying. Here let me fix that."

The purple light returned and then the world went black.

Janine opened her eyes and gasped. Everything was so shiny and bright that she had to squint. "Is this heaven?" she asked, not sure if there was anyone around to answer her.

"No it is not. What is heaven?" the voice said.

"Am I dead?"

"No, you are perfectly healthy now. The ship has analyzed your injuries, corrected them and fixed your blood and organs as well. You will live a long, long time, especially by Earth standards."

She blinked. *The ship? Earth standards?* "Am I on an alien spaceship?" she asked feeling foolish. *What a stupid question!*

He stepped into Janine's line of vision. "Not an alien ship, well at least for me. But I guess yes, for you," he answered.

She gaped at him. She wanted to feel afraid, but she was too awed by the golden alien who stood before her. He was the handsomest creature she'd ever seen, the male of her dreams. Beautiful, and he saved her life. *Well yeah*, she realized, *he did cause the accident, but then he saved me.*

"Are you going to kidnap me?" she asked hopefully, lust stirring inside her. She loved Gerald and the kids, but this was something different.

He laughed.

Oh, what a glorious sound, she thought and shivered with ecstasy.

"I wouldn't kidnap you; it is against all galactic laws. No, I only brought you up here to repair the damage I inadvertently caused. For that, I do apologize. I only popped into your vehicle to have a talk."

"A talk?"

He smiled and the room grew warmer and brightened even more. "Yes, I like to talk to aliens. I find all life forms fascinating, and I'm doing my thesis on alien thought patterns. Earth is famous for the most ridiculous, outlandish ideas."

Janine smiled back at him as her heart fluttered and skipped a few beats. She didn't care what he was saying, she was falling in love with a man from outer space.

"I guess I should get you back," he said his smile fading. "I would have loved to interview you. To get to know you better."

"But . . . but wait," she stammered. "Interview me now. I'm not in a hurry, and this is a chance of a lifetime for both of us."

He nodded, his smile returning, and he said, "Yes, a good idea."

He dropped her off in the field where she'd had the accident. The corn had been replanted in the spring and was ripe and ready for harvest. Tears on her cheeks, Janine waved goodbye to the love of her life and walked to the road to hitch a ride back to town.

Oh, the fuss over her disappearance. They had agreed she should tell an altered truth when she returned, that she'd been abducted by an alien, examined, probed and relentlessly bombarded with questions about her home planet.

She didn't tell anyone the real truth. She never said that they had fallen deeply and completely in love, had explored the galaxy and had a wonderful eleven months improving interplanetary relations.

She was sorry she had abandoned her family like that, but vowed to make it up to them for the rest of her life. After all, she loved her family, she loved Gerald in a quiet comfortable sort of way.

Life for her went on and on and on. Gerald died in front of the TV when he was sixty-one. The kids finally stopped fighting, grew up and gave her lots of grandkids. And she barely aged. At ninety-one, Janine looked forty. That life-saving machine had really improved her health in every way.

Life was all right and she was content, but she always remembered long ago and far away. And she wondered where he was. She often took long rides alone at night. Waiting. Hoping.

And then, one night as she drove next to the cornfields, Janine was blinded by a purple light and heard a loud *pop* next to her. This time she simply pulled over and turned to greet the love of her life.

I'm not saying I ever felt this way, but . . .

LIKE CANDLES ON A CAKE, MAKE A WISH THEN BLOW

"Ready?"

"Yes," Ginny whispered.

Zegragk nodded his bulbous head. "Good."

He lit the thin, greasy candles and sang, "Happy Birthday . . . Happy Birthday, Dear Ginny . . ."

Ginny gasped. The voice of her mother came out from the sizzling tapers and joined in the song.

Tears ran down Ginny's cheeks. "Mom . . . I've missed you . . ."

"Ginny," her mother rasped from the beyond, "Stop slouching, no wonder you're still single. Put on some more weight too, huh?"

Ginny wiped away the tears and blew out the candles, silencing the voice.

"Thanks," she said handing Zegragk some bills. "Just needed my birthday reminder why I killed her."

Sometimes, on a really bad day, life can seem like a horror story.

THE SOUL SUCKERS

The hands! Groping and clawing, the short, soft fingers tried to rip at her. She instinctively knew they were trying to grasp her soul and yank it out.

Glenda woke abruptly, snapping upright on the sofa where she'd been napping. Her body was sweat-soaked and she shuddered at the memory of her recurring nightmare.

"I can't take this anymore," she sobbed, bringing her hands up to cover her face. "What did I do to deserve this?"

A small vindictive voice that lived in her head, her enemy these many years, piped up:

You had the itch,
A wanton bitch,
Sex without fear,
Oh the payment's now dear!

"Shut up!" Glenda shrieked like a B-movie heroine, covering her ears. "Can't you just once make up a decent poem?"

Hush, hush my silly pet, the voice cooed tauntingly, *or a sonnet you will get!*

"Oh, why can't I have a normal conscience?" Glenda moaned. "So I had a wild youth. Everybody was loose back then. Why do I torture myself? It's years too late for guilt."

Suddenly, like the cold winds of Armageddon, she heard an

ominous deep rumble, the very sound from her nightmare. Outside, the vibrations reached for her windows, rattling them, warning her to flee while she had the chance.

Frozen, she stood poised for flight but unable to move. Hissing, the monster belched forth its demons from hell and the air filled with screams.

Panic turned to terror and Glenda's tensed body sprang into action. "Gotta hide," she mumbled. "Gotta get away where they'll never find me!"

Spinning wildly, first one way then the other, Glenda searched for a place of sanctuary. She spotted the basement door but quickly dismissed that dark hole filled with wriggling spiders, fat black water bugs and mildew.

Instead, she turned and ran up the stairs to the second floor. Dashing from room to room, ignoring the dust bunnies nipping at her bare feet and the unmade beds begging to be straightened, she tried to find a place to conceal herself from the approaching creatures. She knew that they were after her, craving her very being, her very self . . . her soul.

Fear clouding her judgment, she dove into the bathtub, cracking her head on the faucets. Stunned, her vision filled with flashes of pain-laced light, she slumped back against the cool porcelain. With eyes crossed, she vaguely watched her blood drip off the end of her nose and mix with the grimy ring adhering to the enamel tub. "Ought to clean in here sometime soon," she mumbled, forgetting for the moment why she was concealed behind the flowery plastic curtain.

Picking up a sour smelling washcloth, she dabbed at the cut on her forehead and tried to recall why she was in a dry bathtub, fully dressed.

"Them!" she shouted as her memory gushed back. "I'm hiding from those bastards who want to suck away my essence." She envisioned herself lying in the tub, an empty, mushy husk of flesh and cellulite, and it made her stomach tighten and her lunch creep up her throat.

"How am I going to survive?" she whimpered, forcing the burning acid back down to the churning storm in her gut.

Why do you ask? her conscience chimed up.

Your fate is your task,
Hiding is your due,
From Demons by you!

"Whoa," Glenda said reviving a bit. "I wish you'd stop telling me that I caused all this. I know I've made mistakes, but cut me a break already! It's bad enough that each time they come for me they want bigger and bigger pieces. Don't te—"

She broke off as the front door downstairs slammed open then shut. Loud footsteps, several sets of them, echoed hollowly as the search started. Powder room, kitchen, living room—she heard them checking the house as they laughed maniacally.

Running feet, heavy feet, drawing ever closer, then pulling away in another direction as voices called her name. They were seeking her out once more, demanding payments for past transgressions.

Fist to her mouth and heart beating rapidly, Glenda held her breath as she heard the fiends retreating down the basement. Too soon they were advancing again, growing louder, drawing closer.

Slowly at first, then faster, they came, running to find their prey, lusting to fill their hunger.

Glenda knew the end was drawing near as she cowered lower. The bathroom door rattled but remained locked. "Please," she sobbed. "Please leave me alone. I'm not ready yet."

Metal scratching on metal; she heard the key slip into the old-fashioned lock and turn with a spirit-shattering click. Glenda covered her eyes with the cloth and stifled a scream as the shower curtain was viciously shoved aside.

She lowered the rag and peeked out at her fate. She saw that their number had grown from two to three. Glenda realized resistance was futile; she sat up and held out her arms to them.

The two familiar ones grabbed her arms and pulled with a strength that almost ripped them from their sockets. The biggest one, whose face was covered by sparse, dark, yet downy hair and red oozing sores, opened his mouth, showing yellowed teeth covered with sharp, flesh-rending metal.

"Ah Mom, quit playing around!" he growled. "We invited Scott for dinner and we're hungry! Are you going to cook something for us soon or what?"

As his words tumbled out, slurred and almost unintelligible, Glenda winced as fiery pain pierced her breast; she felt another piece of her soul being sucked away.

Involuntarily her hands clawed at the phantom pain burning away her identity. Sighing with bitter resignation, she picked up the washcloth, glanced at the three boys and said, "In a minute, I just want to finish cleaning the tub."

This story is a short visit to a post-apocalyptic world where humanity followed different paths.

AS DIFFERENT AS AN ARM AND A LEG

Hube stood in front of the line of dullards. Well, hopefully not all dullards. It was getting harder and harder to fight inbreeding, but still, the fight was his job. And he had to admit that whenever he found that spark of intelligence, it made everything worthwhile: the travel, the wild animals, the stupidity. Yes, almost totally worthwhile.

"Men," he said to his newest troop of volunteers on the first day out. "Men," he repeated while wishing that the Naturals would allow women to join. "I've been to the City and there are many treasures." He held up a package of unopened batteries and a can of peas and waited for the ohs and ahs to subside.

He had done this a dozen times as part of the recruitment traditions. He heard one enlistee say, "My grandmother showed me a bat'ry when I was little. She said it once held great magic inside, but she said she'd been told by her grandmother that monsters took the magic away."

That was three days ago. Now after a journey through the seemingly endless forests, the small group of twenty-seven men huddled together as they approached the city center. The recruits shivered and moaned as they stopped marching and stared at the buildings which were in varying states of decay.

Hube led them to the remains of the department store that held the passageway to his homebase. Without looking back at the trembling mass of fear, stupidity, and hopefully some sort of curiosity, he squeezed through a warped door, then yelled in an excited tone, "Come on in and see what I've found!"

He waited for them to get up the courage to follow him, remembering their slow journey through the dense forests. They'd been on the road less than a day when they'd lost the first recruit to wandering away and another two to careless mistakes. He always lost about ten percent. He hated that part of the job. It was painful, but, then again, it thinned the herd and promoted survival of the fittest. Hube, in his darkest moments, sometimes wondered if the fittest was worth saving anymore, but it was the Cityist tradition to save those that could be saved.

He shook his head in disapproval at himself. He was a purebred Cityist, raised on science and education. He knew many of the Naturals were being converted by people like himself over the last hundred years. Once indoctrinated into the Cityist culture, there was almost no difference between the Tribal Naturals and the purebred City Dwellers.

He thought about this new crew he was bringing in, and smiled when he thought about the blond kid, Marvish. When they were a day out, the kid had said, "Would ya look at that," and pointed to the skeleton of a skyscraper towering above the forest. "What's it?"

Hube nodded with approval, curiosity, always a good sign, then frowned when the 40-year-old man standing next to Marvish grunted. "Bones of a monster. We better turn back. I've been told about the monsters that live in the land of the dead. Evil."

Hube spoke up. "It's just what's left of the City after everyone escaped from the Evil. Come on, we'll be there in a few days. There are no monsters left anymore."

Your ancestors took all of the monsters with them when they abandoned technology to go back to nature, Hube thought. He figured it had probably been a smart idea at the time to have half of the surviving human race flee the technology that had seemed to doom all life on Earth. These Naturals, as they had called themselves, originally believed they were going to turn back the damage 'The Warming' had created.

Unfortunately, the limited gene pool stagnated quickly as the Naturals formed small, isolated tribes and eventually stopped intermingling. He was always amazed how the tribes were so shocked when he showed up, because each tribe didn't know anyone else had survived the rising waters.

The third morning on the move, the troop hit the remains of the highway. Marvish approached it when the rest hung back. He knelt and gingerly touched the road. "Dirt packed so tight it sticks together."

Tellit, a balding man in his thirties, left the huddled group and joined him. "I think a City made this. The Cities must have been something to see."

"Two smart ones," Hube acknowledged with satisfaction. "Come on, just another couple of miles." He led them, most of the men chattering in fear, but the two with curiosity were wide-eyed with wonder as they passed crumbled bridges, collapsed buildings, and twisted metal frames of rusting cars, trucks and trains.

Now, alone inside the department store, Hube wondered how long it would take for someone to follow him. He'd left them outside for at least five minutes when Marvish pushed in and joined him. "The others are afraid. They think the building ate you."

Hube called out to them, "I'm fine. Come see what I've found!"

Tellit came in next, then one by one the others pushed their way inside. Hube hit the light switch and all the men screamed in terror and cowered together. "Fire! Evil!"

"No, electricity," Hube said. "It's just light."

He watched the others stare in fear at the broken mannequins, the smashed counters, the collapsed wall fixtures. Plants and fungus grew everywhere. As one, they all moaned and hugged themselves performing traditional ritualistic gestures. "The Evil!"

Falling to his knees, one yelled, "This place is filled with death. They are all dead here!"

Marvish and Tellit pushed away from the others and picked up the loose arms and legs. "They are hard. Not people at all." Tellit said.

Hube smiled and put his arms around the two. "Welcome to the City, men. Welcome to your new home." He took them through a doorway and down a brightly lit tunnel that led to the new City built into the side of a mountain two centuries ago. After the waters receded, the new habitat had spread to the outside again as a new society rose from the mud. They'd left the ruined old city center as a monument and a reminder of what had happened when the balance between science and nature broke. Then people like Hube started searching for the lost branches of humanity and tried to bring them back to civilization.

Hube nodded. "You two are going to love it here."

As Hube led them away from the group, away from the old traditions of superstition and fear, several Cityists came out from doorways and took the others outside. Hube heard someone say to them, "Come on, it's time to go back home, time to go back to the Natural." He wished that somehow both groups would be able to join together, but he knew deep down that the evolutionary paths they were all following would probably never let it happen. One group to follow its path to devolution, the other growing stronger with the genes of each new recruit. Like the plastic limbs scattered in the abandoned store, humanity was the same as and as different as an arm and a leg.

This story, one that proves moms aren't as dumb as their kids think they are, placed second in "The Cult Of Me" contest in 2015.

~~PAULIE'S~~ HARVEY'S MOM

Paulie's mom studied the clothes, dishes, and fast food wrappers covering the entire bedroom. She took in a breath of sweaty sock odor and said, "Damn, seventeen-years-old and still a pig!"

She walked to the overflowing closet and started digging through games, porn, and sports equipment. Once inside, she saw the small dormer door on the back wall was slightly ajar. She couldn't help but notice there were lights flickering behind it.

She bent low, pushed the door open and saw her son, Paulie, backlit by dozens of candles. He was pouring red liquid onto a large star-like drawing on the wooden floor.

"That better not stain," Paulie's mom shouted. "Go get a bucket and clean this mess up!"

"Ah, Mom!"

"Now!"

As she watched Paulie leave the room, the candles on a makeshift altar blew out with a gust of wind from nowhere. She sighed, and stepping onto the floor drawing, muttered, "I'd give anything to have that boy listen to me!"

"Seriously?" A voice like a hailstorm on a tin roof said. "Anything?"

Paulie's mom looked at the squat figure in the dim light. "Do I know you? You one of Paulie's stoner friends?"

"No," the figure said and relit the candles with a snap of its fingers. "But I think we can get to know each other . . . very well."

Paulie's mom gasped as she took in the huge fangs, the purple, hairy, naked body and the short horns on top of his head. "Oh," she gasped. "You're a . . . a . . ."

"I'm a demon and I can grant your every wish, in exchange for your soul, of course."

"Every wish? Well, maybe . . . I mean . . . Paulie is a nightmare and his father was a womanizing bum. You could punish my husband? Make him suffer?"

The demon smiled, "In ways you can't even imagine."

"Make Paulie finally realize that I'm always right when I tell him to do something?"

"Every word from your lips will be like gospel to him."

Just then Paulie walked in. "Here's your bucket."

I want you to clean up this mess."

"Ah, Mom!" Paulie whined then looked at the demon. "Whoa! It worked. Like, you're mine now, so like, kill my mom for me, okay?"

"Actually, I'm hers now."

Paulie's mom nodded, asking, "Well, you said he'll do everything I tell him?"

"Like gospel."

"Paulie, you know I love you, but I want you to take my place in hell. I don't think my demon . . . uh, what's your name?"

"You can't pronounce it."

"I'll call you Harvey then. Anyway, Harvey won't mind."

"Nope, a soul's a soul."

Paulie frowned. "No way!" he scowled, but was suddenly signing the contract that magically appeared before him.

Then with a scream, he vanished.

"Will he be all right?" she asked feeling a little remorseful.

"Sure," the demon said. "We done now?"

"Well, I need another son. You can take Paulie's place, Harvey."

The demon scowled, "Well, a deal's a deal. By the way, you cook meatloaf?"

"Only the best on Earth," Harvey's mom said. "Now, let's clean up and go eat dinner."

I never forgot the day when I came home from college to find my mother had sold my original Bubble Barbie and the first fuzzy-headed Ken for fifty cents at a yard sale. A trauma like that deserves a story.

ROSES AND IVY

I stood outside the toyshop, rubbing my gloved hands together. It was freezing, but then again, it was Christmas Eve. The last customers left, then I entered.

The wizened, old man behind the counter frowned. He glanced at the clock, three minutes to six, then turned back to watch the TV over the locked glass cabinet behind him.

I smiled and said, "I know it's closing time. I'll only be a few minutes."

He grunted, always the personable salesman. I knew the greedy bastard would stay open till New Year's Eve if it meant making a buck. I walked to the back and stared at the dolls behind those glass doors. I knew every one of them, longed to hold them once again, to own what was rightfully mine. I'd waited five long years to buy my dolls back, and three of them were gone, sold to strangers for exorbitant prices. I hoped their new owners cherished them as much as I had.

The proprietor turned from the TV and divided his time between sizing me up, glancing at the wall clock and studying a hangnail. He absently bit the broken fingernail, spitting it on the floor. "Lovely dolls, aren't they? All collectable, all in perfect condition, all worth a small fortune," he cackled.

I smiled. "Yes, they are beautiful. A young girl would just love to own them, but you are not selling them for a small fortune. No, you are looking to make a huge fortune off of them." I bent and reached under a shelf, lifting up the prize of the entire Rose Doll Collection, Rose's little sister, Ivy. I'd hidden her on the shelf last night when I'd broken into the store. Taking out a cloth from a bag in my coat pocket, I lovingly wiped her down until she gleamed.

He watched me, bit another nail, then realized what I was holding. He stood and squinted at the cabinet display. The Ivy Doll was missing from her stand.

He glared at me, "How'd you get that doll? She's not for sale. She was a limited edition twenty years ago. There are only a few Ivys left in existence!"

"I know," I said as I walked to the counter and put her down. "I just wanted to see her again. She was always my favorite."

He reached for his glasses with one hand and gnawed at his thumbnail of the other, then he grabbed the doll and studied my face. "Ah, I remember you. You're that girlie who tried to have me arrested for stealing your dolls."

"You did."

He laughed, a nasty cackle, and rubbed Ivy across his chin for a moment. "Well, I bought 'em fair from your stepmother, and I think I'll call the police on you now. You broke into my store to get hold of Ivy. Why'd you hide her back there? Why didn't you just take her?"

I smiled. "Because she belongs with the collection. Anyway, you can't prove I broke in, and nothing's missing."

He gnawed on another chipped nail and stared at me. "Just what is it you want? It's past closing. What kind of mind game you playing here?"

I smiled, "I like that, mind game. Exactly!" Then I nodded, laid three one-hundred dollar bills on the counter and went to the door.

"Merry Christmas. You should change these cheap locks."

I watched him put Ivy back in the case, then he grabbed the money and shouted, "What's this for?"

I didn't answer, I just clasped my gloved hands together and left thinking, *Yeah* . . . .

I walked ten blocks to the hospital, my coat barely keeping me warm, but my accomplishment was like a furnace for my soul. Once there, I headed to the back, and using my key, unlocked the large toxic waste receptacle and threw in my thrift-shop gloves and coat with the baggie still in the pocket. My latex gloves lining my wool gloves followed. The dumpster was half empty, and by tomorrow night it would be teeming from all the holiday accidents and emergencies, and the day after that, it would be emptied.

Yes, this Christmas was for me and Dad, God rest his soul. A decade ago, that vicious witch married him for his money, then discovered he was just a poor, sick man with a teenage daughter.

I went off to college and she sold everything we owned, including the house. She even sold my Rose doll collection for three hundred dollars. Dad used to buy me a doll every Christmas and birthday. I loved them so much, and had planned to give them to my daughters when I had a family.

That bitch ran off, and Dad died penniless. I struggled and worked and finally graduated nursing school. What a shock when my stepmother ended up in the ER on my shift last Christmas Eve, just like a present. Poor woman died. I mean, who could've known she was allergic to penicillin?

This year, I worked in the infectious disease ward, and decided to give myself another Christmas present. My little Ivy, wiped with the cloth that had been soaked in all sorts of deadly germs and bacteria, had become Poison Ivy for the night. That nail biting creep should be feeling pretty sick about now.

By the end of my shift, he'll be dead and no one will even know he was murdered. I smiled at the thought. Wow, another easy death and I'm the only one who will ever know it, just my own little mind crime. I'll pop on over to the shop tomorrow to collect and disinfect my purchases. It will be good to have my Roses and Ivy back home for the holidays.

What if the entire universe were as stupid as mankind?

THE WAY WE WERE

Jack was almost asleep. He'd been sitting at this seat for thirty years waiting, hoping, for just a sign, any sign of intelligent life out there.

Suddenly static brought him awake. What luck . . . Contact on his watch!

"Greetings," a metallic voice said. "Fear not your future, for we know all and wish to share."

Jack listened, recording this momentous occasion.

"Al Gore wins in 2000, Prince Charles gets back with Diana, and Britney Spears becomes the greatest star ever born on your planet."

Jack sighed with bitterness and snapped off the recorder. Another false alarm, still no intelligent contact!

I am so proud of this story. It won first place in the 1991 Scavenger's Newsletter Killer Frog contest. My first writing award! Killer Frog stories are silly and deliberately over-done, b-movie horror and let me tell you, trying to write absurd horror was difficult but the results are good for a laugh.

DARN THEM

As I write this, my last testament, I am hiding on this uncharted tropical island awaiting my doom to find me. Although I know I've hidden my trail well, to "them" it's probably as clear as footprints in the sands of time. It's not that I am a coward, but after reading my tale you'll understand why I've got cold feet.

I only ask that whoever finds this bottle will take my story to the proper authorities or call it in to the *National Enquirer*. After all, I and my late lover, Shirley, discovered a secret so protected and shrouded in mystery, that since the time mankind first became civilized enough to wear more than a bearskin, we have all been searching for the answer. Well, I have that answer and I am going to share it with you, whoever you may be, only . . . only remember the knowledge can be fatal, and Lord knows how many innocent victims have already choked on the secret.

But, alas, I am rambling on and on like a run in a bad pair of pantyhose. It's just so lonely here all by myself. I wish I had someone to talk to, but where there are people there's clothing, so I stay alone and alive until the day they come and sock it to me.

It all started last month when Shirley and I went to the Jersey Shore for a weekend of salty sun and fun. Early Saturday morning we woke to find the day steel gray, overcast and as cold as my last wife. The beach we had picked was not popular anyway, and on this day it was as empty as my underwear drawer on laundry day.

"Come on Shirley," I said to the woman I loved. "This place costs too much to stay inside. I paid for two days at the beach and damn it, we're going to the beach."

Shirley cringed and shot me a dirty look; she hated when I cursed, so I apologized. Never has an expletive ever passed those ruby lips.

And so, we dressed in our swimsuits, packed a picnic lunch and went down to the beach. There we sat, shivering on our lobster towels, when a large wave roared up to our feet. As it hissed backwards, retreating to join the main force before it would charge again, we started to laugh. At the edge of the towels lay three, bedraggled, sandy socks discarded by the now soulless sea.

"Look," I said, "three unmatched socks. I wonder where their partners are?"

Teeth chattering, Shirley managed an ever so dainty giggle. "Maybe they're the ones that always escape from the washing machines."

I could see she was warming to the subject, but I suddenly felt a cold wind blow at my soul.

"Maybe they all just slip out of the machines though the pipes, and flow through the sewers until they reach the freedom of the open seas," she said. "Maybe all the partner-less socks in the whole wide world come here to—"

"Shirley, drop it!" I barked, suddenly as afraid as a bicyclist on a six-lane highway at rush hour. Something was nagging at me and somehow, I knew Shirley was treading on dangerous ground. I looked at those socks, and I could swear they were closer to us. "Look honey, it's too cold for this. Let's go back to our room and watch cartoons or something."

Shirley looked at me with an adorable cross-eyed expression but agreed. As we walked back over the dunes, I noticed several more socks strewn randomly on the sand. *Something is up here*, I thought. *Could Shirley be onto something?*

Just a Drop in the Cup

We spent the day watching Saturday afternoon monster movies on the TV, eating chips and making love. It could have been the most perfect day of my existence, but . . . but this wonderful day turned out to be our undoing. As I look back now, I can see how our lives swiftly unraveled.

Sometime near dinnertime I dozed off and Shirley, ah sweet, beautiful Shirley, according to the note she had left me, went out in search of a sandwich shop. When I woke the room was dark and the wind was high. I looked out the window of our shaky shore cottage to see a leaden sky as gray as my car after a month of water restrictions. Dusk was almost upon us and lightning flashed in the distance. The wind was whipping stray raindrops into the wet sand, and the dunes were black.

"Black?" I muttered and squinted to see better. The sand was covered by dark ominous shapes. Shapes, evil in their obscurity. Shapes, writhing and slithering in the sand and brush. Shapes, long and thin. Shapes in search of something.

Terrified, I remembered my blond, beautiful Shirley was somewhere out there. I prayed she wasn't on the beach. Gathering all my courage, I opened the door and went out to find my love. I was prepared to wade through a beach full of snakes to find her, prepared to wade to hell and hopefully back, but I wasn't prepared for what I found.

Up the dunes I trudged, looking for a stick to beat off any stray reptiles. The shapes burrowed into the soft, wet sands as I approached and I crossed the dunes effortlessly heading toward the choppy, churning Atlantic.

I walked silently and as I neared the flat white expanse of sand leading to the water, I saw a sight that would knock your socks off—permanently. There in front of me were about seventy socks, and none of them matched. They were in every size from child to bigfoot and in colors ranging from basic dress black to pink and lavender stripes. There were sweat socks and argyle socks, and they were alive.

Alive! Alive and moving, slithering like the snakes I had mistaken them for. I stopped, held my breath and hoped they wouldn't attack me.

I was ignored, for they were in the midst of a mating frenzy. All around me, socks had paired off. Joining each other, the bottom lay flat on the sand and the second one climbed on top and covered it. Then the bottom one stretched open its top and swallowed the two of them. Looking like a normal pair of folded socks, they rolled over and over until they hit the cold surf and separated. It made me sick until I realized that now they were probably hungry.

Nausea was quickly replaced with fear. My stomach was trying to push itself inside out like one of those neatly folded socks as I watched a low flying sea gull get snatched out of the air. One moment it was soaring toward the dunes, and the next moment a dark coiled sock sprang off the sand and quickly wrapped itself around the bird's neck. The gull panicked and wobbled lower. Another sock uncoiled, flying thought the air to join the first. Then a third. It ended with a squawk and a loud snap as the bird plummeted to the beach, its neck broken by the trio of knitted yarn's stranglehold.

As soon as the bird hit, the rest of the horde converged, covering it in a blanket of hungering wool and rayon. Two minutes later, they moved off into the water, swimming to the ocean's depths, leaving a small pile of bird bones and a handful of feathers to blow in the wildly swirling wind.

Shirley!

Where was Shirley? I screamed out her name, fearing the worst. They attacked me then. I hadn't seen the five sentinels left lying on the sand off to my right. Latching onto my ankle, they wrapped themselves up my leg, wrapping and wrapping to move themselves higher. I grabbed at them, ripping them off and tearing them apart with my hands and teeth. Howling triumphantly at the lightning flashing across the ink black sky, I threw their tattered remains to the ground.

The sky, in a dramatic burst of electricity, lit up as if in acknowledgement of my victory, or perhaps in a flash of ironic humor, for I saw her then. She lay half on the sand, half in the surf, bobbing gently on the tiny waves.

I fell to my knees and crawled to her. Dragging her body to land, I

Just a Drop in the Cup

cradled her in my lap. I wiped the caked sand from her face and hair, and wept. Her head hung limply at an unnatural angle. I thought she was dead.

Her beautiful eyes suddenly fluttered open, and she gave me a weak smile. "They got me because I was right," she rasped.

Tears fell from my eyes as I tried to keep her still. "Hush," I whispered. "Save your strength."

"Too l . . . l . . . late!" She gurgled and rattled. "Save yourself and warn the world!" Struggling to take in a last breath, she heaved a sad sigh and closed her eyes.

"Shirley!" I bellowed with an agony that felt worse than being financially wiped out by my third wife.

She opened her eyes and looked annoyed. "What?" She managed to gasp.

"Nothing," I answered, "I just thought you were dead."

"N . . . not yet." Her eyes grew wide and round, and she grimaced with pain. "Now I am." Her body stiffened with a spasm and she whispered in so soft a voice I almost missed it, "Darn them. Darn those socks!"

And she died.

Holding my dead lover, I sat on that dark beach as the rain beat upon us. I suddenly thought about all the socks I had worn for the last thirty-seven years, all those parasitic socks living off my sweat. I bet they weren't absorbing my perspiration. I bet they were drinking it, building up their strength on my excreted minerals until they were strong enough to make that long escape Shirley had joked about. I couldn't help but wonder if socks had socklets, and did they all live in the seas, attacking random swimmers and dragging them under to feast upon them?

Then the realization hit me and I knew my doom was sealed. I had discovered the answer to two of mankind's most perplexing mysteries. I not only discovered where all the missing socks of the world went, I figured out what happened to all those ships and sailors that vanished in the Bermuda Triangle. The socks got them! That had to be the answer, and I knew that they were not only capable of killing to protect their secret, I also knew it was only a matter of time before they found out the sentinels had failed and they'd come after me.

I dropped Shirley on the sand and ran. I ran like a greyhound racing after that fake rabbit, like a purse-snatcher running from Superman, like an Olympian hopeful on enhancement drugs. I ran until I got to this place.

So here I am, hiding out and hopefully delivering my message to the world. Please believe me, what I have written is no wild yarn. I only hope someone finds this bottle before "they" do. Nothing would make me feel more like a heel than to think my story would be lost, dragged to oblivion by the undertoe!

And here's a short whodunit about the death of a millionaire who had an interesting sense of humor.

DIG IT!

The reading of Gregory Xavier's will was quick. It read: *To all the bloodsuckers, you must all watch this video and follow the directions exactly or leave now and forfeit all.*

I looked around the room. All six chairs were filled. I was invited to watch, but I wasn't allowed to sit; I was still on Gregory's payroll. I served coffee then stood in the corner.

Elmer Harris turned on the huge television and we watched, the seven of us: Elmer, Gregory's first wife Tiffany, his second wife Bambi, his third wife Charlotte, Timothy, who was Tiffany's idiot son, Nicole, Bambi's bitch-in-training and me, Gail Zimmer, the housekeeper. The two homicide detectives back by the door didn't count.

I eyed the group as they watched Gregory's handsome image on the screen. I studied them instead of him, because they were always a wonder to observe and because it still hurt to see Gregory. I missed him so much.

Gregory's voice pierced my hearing. "... of sound mind and body do bequeath...ah, screw that. You all want to know what I'm leaving you. Well, Elmer, you've been gouging me for years as my bloodsucking lawyer, but as my best friend, I leave you my library of rare books and games and my Corvette collection."

The three ex-wives and children groaned at that news and mumbled to each other.

"I worked hard, made my fortune playing games," Gregory continued from the great beyond. "It seems the only game I couldn't win was the game of life, because if this recording is playing, I'm obviously dead. It appears you can't beat genetics. Kids, as you carelessly waste your youth, know this: you probably have all my cancer genes. Consider them a pass go and collect death freebee from your dear, old dad."

I stood there fighting my tears. I was really going to miss that man! I guess in some ways he will always be with me, but that wasn't going to keep me warm at night. I held the five envelopes so tightly in my fisted hands, they crumpled. I listened to the rest of the recording as I tried to un-wrinkle the papers.

"So, I'm sure none of you will begrudge me one last game: a round of treasure hunt! Each of you will receive clues, and if you follow them, you will all get a special surprise. Gail, give everyone their shovels and, of course, a map."

Before he had even stopped speaking, the herd of vultures were grabbing at the envelopes. In a flash they were all shoving each other to get outside first. I watched the three wives in their designer black dresses and four-inch heels rush through the huge French doors to the back patio and terraced gardens. They tottered out to find the line of golden shovels and started to dig up the perfectly maintained grounds. The two spawn were right behind them.

The two detectives watched as well, not even hiding their grins. I overheard one say, "Finding suspects in this case is just too easy."

"Coffee, gentlemen?" I said to Elmer and the police. We retired to the elevated patio overlooking the gardens and took in the chaos below.

"Do you know who killed him?" I asked as we watched dirt flying in arcs all over the place.

"We don't know yet, but the IV was pure poison, a weed killer." one detective said. "Shame we don't have the body, but, either way, it was a stupid and obvious murder. Crude and sloppy. I'd put my money on any of those buffoons down there."

We all turned to watch the five treasure hunters digging up the gardens and lawn, apparently so blinded by greed they were not even capable of following clues.

After an hour in the midday heat, the five heirs returned to the patio with locked treasure chests. I had keys and handed them out. Tiffany, Bambi and Charlotte ripped them from my hand without a thank you and opened their chests.

I enjoyed the expression on their faces as they each took out a large velvet bag filled with gold nuggets. Their smiles melted away as each read the paper under the bag. FOOLS GOLD FOR EACH OF MY GOLD-DIGGING WIVES.

Timothy and his half-sister grabbed their keys right after their mothers. Opening his chest, Timothy recoiled. A stinking, dead rabbit rotted on the bottom. His note read: A HARE FOR MY HEIR.

Nicole fared no better when she discovered a sack of apple seeds and a note reading: FOR THE FRUIT OF MY LOINS, THE APPLE OF MY EYE.

They grumbled, then ranted until I decided enough was enough. "Please get off my patio. In fact, get off my property."

As their voices rose to a deafening cacophony of disbelief, I held up my sack filled with keys. I also waved the note that came with it: TO MY LOYAL, LOVING HOUSEKEEPER, I LEAVE THE KEYS TO MY HOUSE AND HEART.

House wasn't exactly the correct term, it was a mansion, but I wasn't going to argue. I never argued with Greg. I loved him too much. I looked toward the detectives. They nodded and escorted everyone off my property.

Quiet descended.

I knew who killed Gregory.

No one!

He decided on one last game, an IV switch after he died to stir things up, to make his wives and children suspects and hopefully miserable. The doctor was called in, took one look at the body and the IV bag with the wrong color fluid and ordered an autopsy and a police investigation. Then the body mysteriously disappeared on the way to the morgue. I knew Gregory had to be laughing on the other side.

At dusk, I left for the warehouse we bought a few weeks back. I needed to check that everything was running correctly. Amid all the machines, Gregory was there, frozen, waiting for the cure.

You see, Gregory was the ultimate game player. Sure that he could win the game of life, he put his chips on coming back alive.

And me, I'll be waiting in our mansion, betting he will, too.

This started out as a writing exercise about aliens, conquest, and coffee. It grew into a fun and totally absurd story.

JUST A DROP IN THE CUP

Nothing's like the smell of fresh coffee in the morning, afternoon or evening. Heck, a good cup of coffee on a restless night is just the cure for tossing and turning and fighting the pillow. It'll get ya right out of that bed.

My life had been dedicated to the stuff. Just to smell it made my mouth water, and the thought of all that caffeine made my heart beat faster. Don't tell my wife, but sometimes I think a good cup of coffee excites me more than a beautiful woman, and at my age it lasts longer than sex, too.

I loved the brew so much that when I retired from the food processing lab, I opened my own neighborhood coffee shop. Oh, it started out small, but it grew. By the third year, I had to expand to a bigger site.

I sold coffee, all kinds of coffee, but it was all real coffee. Every drink, whether frozen, steamed or brewed was made with my own blend. It had taken a while, but after much experimentation and a bit of minor augmentation, I had created what, in my opinion, was the world's best cup of coffee. And by all the customers who came in droves just to get some, I was pretty sure I was right, even if it wasn't actually one hundred percent coffee.

Just as I thought everything was perfect, Bark House Coffee started sending their corporate dogs to sniff around. Yeah, that's right, Bark House Coffee had heard about my local business and had come to edge me out.

It's not bad enough that everywhere you turn, whether at the airport, the train station, a theme park, the turnpike and just about every other street corner, there was always one of those stinking pseudo-log cabins selling plastic coffee in plastic cups. And their dumb slogan, *Quaint little coffee shops that bring the world of international coffee right to your hometown*, annoyed the hell outta me, too.

Before I knew it, they were building a Bark House Coffee Shoppe right down the street from me. Well, I wasn't all that worried; after all, my coffee was the real thing, and theirs was corporate sludge covered up with fancy flavors.

But a week after they opened, my business dropped off.

"Just a fluke," I told myself. "Not to worry, they'll be back after the novelty wears off."

Only, I was wrong. The customers didn't return, they just continued dropping off. After a month, I started to get concerned. I had been sure my regulars were going to return, but they didn't. By the second month I was in financial trouble. By the third month, I was digging into my nest egg and I was beyond angry.

I was royally screwed by American big business corporations . . . wait, make that global corporations . . . or better yet, I wouldn't be far off at all if I said universal.

I decided to see for myself what was so appealing about this Bark House Coffee. I went over one afternoon and the place was jammed. People everywhere drinking lattes, espressos, cappuccinos, frozen concoctions, hot concoctions, and everything in between.

I ordered a coffee, black. At first sip it tasted weak and had a strange afterbite, but by the third sip, I liked it. A lot. Hell, I even liked the plastic log cabin motif.

Just a Drop in the Cup

After I left, the feeling wore off and all I had was a nasty aftertaste in my mouth along with the bitter taste of resentment.

How odd, I thought. *Why did I think that that gunk tasted good?* I needed to do some serious research to find out. Later that night, I broke into the Bark House. Actually, I just hid in the basement and waited till they closed.

At midnight, I crawled out of my hiding place. The basement was completely empty except for a large raised circular platform in the middle of the floor. There were no supplies, equipment or anything. I searched the entire building; I couldn't find any sacks of coffee, or anything else.

I just got back to the basement to wait for opening time when the platform lit up and started humming. The light hurt my eyes even as I hid behind a wall partition. I didn't want to do it, but I squeezed them shut against the brightness.

When I opened them again, the basement was filled with dogs. Dogs! Barking at each other, standing upright and unloading coffee supplies from the platform. I was confused and frightened. The lead dog hit a button on his belt and held up a paw. Suddenly, he stopped barking and was speaking English. "Communicators on, set to America."

All the dogs stopped what they were doing and hit their communicators.

I wasn't frightened anymore; I was scared beyond belief. They all hit another button and they shimmered and became humans. The humans came in every color, shape and sex.

"Just like their Halloween," one of them said. "Stupid holiday!"

"Yeah," the leader agreed. "Well, in a couple more years we will have total mind control of the species and we can do away with all their nonsense. Just wait until the planet is ours and the humans are our pets."

As soon as they unloaded and opened the store, I snuck out and ran home. I wasn't frightened or scared anymore. Hell no, I was pissed off. How dare they take over our world by brainwashing us with tainted coffee! How dare they ruin the only drink I ever truly loved!

I decided to fight them the only way I could. I closed my coffee shop and moved to another city. Yep, this is the third healthfully, wholesome, rejuvenating tea room I've opened this year. If my plan works, my special teas, which are now just as addictive as Bark House Coffee, will catch on even bigger. Soon my teas will replace coffee worldwide, and then Bark House and their plans of world domination can just go back to the dogs!

After reading three long, holiday newsletters that arrived in holiday cards one afternoon, I just absolutely had to write one of my own.

THAT HOLIDAY NEWSLETTER

Hi, All Important Family Members and Dear, Dear Friends:

Well, it's that time once again when I know, if you are at all like me, you look so forward to these long personal Christmas letters. I'm sure that you eagerly make time to read every word during the mad holiday rush. Although this year has been very, very eventful and incredibly full for my entire family, I wouldn't want to disappoint anyone and not get our annual letter out. So have cheer, I managed to sit down and get this one done in time.

January:

The new year began with great things looming. I started working full time at the mall. I am making 20 cents above minimum wage at a coffee kiosk and the future looks bright. Stu (my husband, for all you who have forgotten I got married two decades ago), is still looking for a job, but the prospects are looking up on that front as well. As you all remember from last year, Stu was let go and has been diligently seeking employment for the last fourteen months. The boys and I have been very supportive in this search and we realize that a man of Stu's intelligence cannot settle for just any sort of job, but must find a position.

But have no fear for us, with my new job and all the overtime I get, once again our house is safe and we have food on the table most of the time. Both boys, Andy and Manny, went to school every day, not missing once due to sickness, even though I normally would have kept Manny home with that gunky, green eye infection and all. I don't have any sick days yet at work, so even with a fever of 102, I figured that he's still better off in school learning and socializing with all his classmates then home alone playing games on his computer.

February:

Worked all month. Andy spent an evening at the emergency room for an ear infection and needed drops twice a day for two weeks! It was touch and go the entire time on whether he'd remember those drops, but we were so proud of him because he only forgot to use them twice. He's such a mature and responsible young man now and we are looking forward to him graduating this year. Last year's confusion over all those days the school had wrongly marked him absent is behind us, and we are sure that Andy didn't mind the extra year of education.

For Valentine's Day, Stu took me to Atlantic City on a casino bus where we enjoyed an almost free buffet. Stu won a hundred dollars on the five dollars that we got free, which was great since I somehow misplaced my paycheck earlier in the week. I was impressed at how long Stu was able to make that five dollars last before he hit the hundred dollars. I lost my five bucks in about a minute, but he was able to keep playing and playing. It seemed like he was putting money in the machine all the time, but since he only had the five dollars it had to be an illusion. I mean where else could he have gotten money to gamble?

March:

Had my birthday, and yes, I still celebrate them. We all went out for a special birthday dinner at McDonald's, and I even got a sparkler in my yogurt dessert. Stu, as always, remembered everything to make my day special. He even bought me a new wool coat; well, I think semi-new since it had a wad of used tissues in the pocket. At the end of the month we got the best news of all: Stu finally found a great job and now all our worries are over! I've contacted our lawyer, Larry, and stopped the bankruptcy proceedings just in the nick of time. We are sure that this job will be the one to carry Stu to retirement. I'm so happy for him, what with all those other dead-end jobs he had to suffer through year after year. It is so tough to be appreciated in this world and at last, this year, Stu will finally get his due.

April:

The boys had a wonderful spring break. They stayed home all week and cleaned their rooms. I am definitely blessed with such wonderful boys, so I paid them one hundred dollars each for being so industrious. Sometimes when I look at them, I see them both growing up to be just like their father.

Manny worked the whole month on his science fair project, growing leafy plants and drying out the leaves. He kept me busy buying plastic snack bags, but I'm sure he will get an A on whatever his project was.

May:

We had a close one this month. Stu got a splinter in his finger and it wouldn't come out. Poor Stu. Oh, how he suffered, couldn't help with any of the house or yard work for two weeks.

I was so proud of Stu; he was so very brave throughout the entire ordeal, although he used up all his paid sick days for the rest of the year.

Once he was better, he took on the job of fixing my car, Louis. Stu told me that after ten years, a car should have a complete tune up, and why should we spend all that money on it when he is perfectly capable of doing it himself? Am I lucky to have married such a versatile man or what?

June:

Louis, my car, and I were in an accident. I was all right thanks to my seatbelt, although strangely enough the airbag failed to deploy. I still don't know what happened. All of a sudden I was off the road and into the trees. Lucky for me I had decided to take the long way to work instead of the cliff road.

Louis had to be out of commission for six weeks and the insurance company tried to total him, but Stu stepped in and said that this was my car, and damn it, I deserved to keep him. Stu managed to get the parts we needed and Louis is almost as good as new. He pulls to the right and the brakes slip about fifty percent of the time, but Stu insists that it isn't really dangerous at all and that I shouldn't worry. I'm so lucky to have married a man as caring as Stu. He always makes me feel safe.

School ended and, sadly, Andy somehow forgot about his graduation ceremony and we all missed it. But he said not to worry because the principal would send him his diploma during the summer. Both boys are happy to be home. They are busy catching up on their sleep and I find I have to wake them when I get home to make dinner. Kids . . . gosh they never change.

July:

We used our brand-new portable charcoal bar-b-que grill repeatedly in July. I couldn't believe that Stu had actually gone to the store and got it for our anniversary! Is my man thoughtful or what? Thanks to that grill, we ate hotdogs and burgers almost every night. I just love a grilled hunk of red meat with a side of corn smothered in butter and a baked potato topped with sour cream and melted cheddar cheese with real bacon bits. We ate such healthy, well-balanced meals all month.

August:

Manny was so industrious that he kept his spring science project going and now has fourteen of those leafy plants in the backyard. He is such a good farmer.

Andy went out several times this summer to collect money door to door for the Scouts. It came as surprise to me because I didn't even know he joined the Scouts and I thought he'd be a little old for that, being nineteen and all, but my sons are always a constant source of pride for me. Children are always full of pleasant surprises, and the Scouts must be so happy to get all the cash he raised.

September:

Well, back to school month again and Andy told us he signed up for classes at the community college. I was so glad that he took those two classes that we told him he needn't find a job. College must be very different than high school because it seems to me that his two classes are constantly meeting on different days and at different times. I found that he sometimes even had go to school on Saturday night.

Manny has taken up playing games on his new game system and even bought a new fifty-five-inch smart TV. When I asked him where he got the money, he said he found an afterschool job. And I had thought he had been home after school every day doing his homework. What a great kid, getting a job as well as keeping up with his schoolwork.

Stu started working overtime once the autumn hit. He stayed late almost every night trying to get an important project finished on deadline. It was so good to see him happy with his job. He came home after midnight every evening and although he was too tired to even kiss me goodnight, he was very happy.

October:
Stu went off on a business trip with a special new friend from work. They are spending lots of time together, but Stu said it was a busy time with the new project and he had to put in even more night and weekend work. I was glad his new coworker, Sheila, was there at his side so he didn't feel lonely at the office. In fact, as soon as their schedule slows down, I'm going to fix Sheila up with my cousin Tony.

I also discovered that Andy had a special little girlfriend, because he was constantly on the phone all night with her. Sometimes I'd overhear their conversations and I'd get such a kick out of hearing him moan, "Oh baby," over and over. How cute!

November:
Great news. I earned a free turkey at the supermarket, so we had Thanksgiving dinner at home for the first time in years. It was a shame Stu had to work all weekend, but I saved him leftover turkey and he said it was great. We had a mystery here at home. Our phone/internet bill was $978.00. I know I made a few calls to a psychic network just to be sure that Stu wasn't doing anything he'd regret with Sheila, but I certainly didn't go to the *Hot Babes in Bikinis* site. We are working

with the credit card company to have them remove those fraudulent charges since they couldn't have possibly been made from here.

December:

Well, it has been an entire year of thrills and excitement and here we are, almost at the holidays again. But what an eventful month December has been.

Sadly, Manny was arrested in school for selling pot. I have no idea where he got the stuff, but when he gets out, I'm sure he will have learned his lesson. After all, he has always been a good and smart boy.

The phone company continued to bill us for Hot Babes in Bikinis. Hopefully, our lawyer, Larry, when he gets back from vacation, will be able to clear that up, because, although I may have turned a slightly blind eye to the boys' antics, they are still and always will be my sons.

Stu has had it rough as well. He lost his job for stealing, and it appears Sheila, who has mysteriously vanished, was embezzling huge sums of money from the company. Stu said she framed him.

Worst of all, it appeared that someone took Louis for a joyride and his brakes completely failed and he went over a cliff. Unfortunately, he burst into flames and when the wreck was recovered, there was a headless woman's body wrapped in what was left of my birthday coat inside the trunk. Stu has been arrested for the embezzled money and the mysterious body in the trunk.

On the plus side of all this, I am hoping that he can bond more with Manny now that they have criminal records in common.

As for me, as you've probably read in the papers or saw on the news, I'm probably dead, my murdered, headless body discovered in that accident. And, even if by some chance, that slut Sheila was the body in the trunk instead of me, and I'm really still alive somewhere on a tropical island with Stu's missing company funds that I accidentally found in Stu's trunk, and I'm there with Larry, our lawyer, well, then I'll be really, really busy taking notes for the next eleven months so I can keep everyone abreast of our special little family.

Happy Holidays to Everyone.

Jill

I just love writing drabbles and this one came to mind late one night.

A SMALL, BROWN PLANET TO CALL HOME

Colonizing Mission Log

Day 5,321: Our race, ready to breed, cannot find a suitable planet to call home. The Captain is worried.

Day 5,412: We're getting desperate. We cannot nest inside this ship. If we don't give birth in the open atmosphere, we will die.

Day 5,438: The scouting team discovered a brown planet. It's perfect. Obviously once inhabited, covered with decaying, tall, structures, it now appears abandoned. The seas have a perfect jelly-like consistency for us to nest on and the air is thick.

Day 5,445 We are saved and now call this third planet from their sun our home.

People who read some of my stories ask me if I'm happily married. Yes, I really, really, really am. I just enjoy writing about people who really, really, really are not. This story is a bit longer then it was in the original book to add to the suffering.

SO SORRY . . . BUT . . .

Bob Schwartz stood at the edge of the Grand Canyon and spread his arms wide in an all-encompassing manner. He turned to smile at his brand-new wife.

"Ain't nature grand!" he called, even though she was only an arm's length away.

Lucinda Jones-Middleton-McDonald-O'Hara-Schwartz gazed at Bob as he turned back to stare at the wide-open spaces before him. She shivered and hugged herself. *God, I love this man.* She smiled as she stared at his back and thought about how easy it would be to give him one little push. No one was around and she was sure he was just waiting for her to slip up, show her true colors.

"No wait," she said softly, "not Bob. Bob loves me, and I love him."

I found the perfect husband this time, she thought as she suddenly reached out with both hands and, without even realizing it, shoved him.

Bob half turned toward her and teetered, his arms pinwheeling wildly, a stricken look on his normally handsome face.

"Oh, my God! What . . ." she screamed. She hadn't meant to do that! It was just a reflex, a random act with no thought, no malice.

Just a Drop in the Cup

As he fell backward, Lucinda screamed. "Bob! Oh Bob. I'm so sorry." She ran to the edge and fearfully looked over. A wave of light-headed relief washed over her. She saw Bob right below her desperately hanging onto a stunted tree growing on the cliff face.

"Bob," she shouted again, horrified that she had actually pushed him. "Bob, I'm so sorry."

He clung to the bush. "Why . . . why'd you do this?"

"I'm sorry, I . . . I didn't mean it!" She cried and dropped flat on the dirt, stretching out her arms over the edge in a desperate attempt to grab him.

He reached up with first one hand and as she clasped it, he grabbed with the other. She grunted with the effort and tried to pull him up but, even with all her weight training at the gym, he was too heavy. She lay there on the dry, sandy ground as sweat beaded on her forehead and trickled down into her eyes.

Blinking away the burning drops of perspiration, wishing she could use her hands to rub the briny pain away, Lucinda whimpered, "I was so sure that I could make it work this time."

Her head and shoulders protruded over the edge. She felt tears well up and saw them fall, splashing onto his upturned face, leaving streaks in the dirt on his cheeks.

As they held onto each other, his hands locked around her wrists and her hands locked around his, he said, "Lucy, I don't understand. This wasn't an accident."

She didn't answer, shame filling her with guilt.

"You . . . you really killed your other four husbands . . . didn't you?" Bob asked as he struggled to cling to her like a trapeze acrobat.

Lucinda still didn't answer. She felt the mask of innocence and emotional fragility shift momentarily to show the killer underneath, then it settled back into place once again.

She recalled how her first husband, a violent, abusive drunk, had lost control of his car and went over a cliff. She'd never even been suspected for that one. Oh, it hadn't been planned, not really. They'd left the bar that night, the bar that was a long mountainous road away from home, and he'd passed out cold in the driver's seat before he even turned the key. She stared at him for a short time, touched the healing bruises on her cheek and set his dead-weight foot against the gas petal. Then she turned the ignition on and let him and the car speed out of sight on that twisty road.

The police found her limping, covered in dirt and crying. They accepted her story about him pushing her from the car and taking off without her. Everyone accepted her story; everyone knew he was an alcoholic and said how lucky she was to not have been in the car that night.

And when guilt started to set in, she had reasoned it wasn't really murder. It was self-defense.

Her second husband, another bully, had died in a hunting accident. She'd supposedly been miles away, but she'd actually been close enough to pull the trigger. By the time they came to tell her about it, she'd been back home for an hour. This time there was no guilt because she knew without a doubt that it wasn't murder when it was self-defense.

Then there was her third husband, a nice man with a betting problem who had squandered more than half the insurance money from the first two husbands. Sadly, he'd fallen down the basement stairs and replenished the coffers at the same time. Again, self-defense as she needed his insurance money to replace what he'd squandered.

By the time she'd married her fourth husband, people were beginning to whisper that perhaps she suffered from more than incredible marital misfortune. Unfortunately, he was an incurable bore who was known to suffer from bouts of depression. It was so sad when he took an overdose of sleeping pills and antidepressants. This time, for sure it was self-defense because he was killing her with boredom.

She knew some people thought she was a murderer, a black widow, but she had always been clever and careful and hid everything well. She was always in control.

That was where Bob came in, reporter for the local paper, trying to make a name for himself with a story that could go national. Instead, he made a name for her, giving her a ring and another hyphen. This time she knew she could give up her murderous ways and was ready to settle into her new, wonderful life with a wonderful husband.

But, now as Lucinda clung to Bob, she'd realized that maybe, just maybe, she was hooked on murder and couldn't stop. Her arms were burning; they felt like they were being pulled from their sockets, and her shoulders were sending jolts of pain into her neck, but she held on. The sun beat down and they were both sweating heavily. Lucinda felt Bob's hands sliding from her wrists, inching toward her fingers.

"Lucy!" he called. "Please, don't let me die!"

Flat on the ground, holding onto the man she'd just married, Lucinda suddenly realized, with a wave of relief, that she wasn't a cold-blooded murderer. Why, he'd probably turn me in if we stayed together. He'd write that story and become a big-time reporter just like he always said he wanted to be.

She shook her head and screamed at him, "You're using me!"

And let go.

His grip faltered as their sweat soaked hands slid apart and then he was falling.

"Oh Bob," she called down to his dwindling body. "Why'd you force me to do this?"

After a while she stood up, tears still running down her cheeks. *Well, this is the last time*, she decided, *the last time I'm ever going to be victimized by a man.* She brushed at the dirt on her shirt, looked around and started screaming. "Help me! Help, my husband tripped and fell! Someone, anyone? Help!"

She waited, knowing that help would eventually come. Yes, she knew people would talk, she was sure of that, but she'd be proven a hapless victim of circumstances once again. A woman destined to always be a widow.

She also knew that men would still keep marrying her anyway.

A flashback to my single days in the disco nights of the late 1970's. I too tried to wait for my knight but ended up in the real world instead.

SOME DAY MY KNIGHT WILL COME

"Grandma?"

"Yes, Ginny?" I replied.

"Grandma, tell me how you and Grandpa met, fell in love, and lived happily ever after."

"Again?"

I watched Ginny nod her head vigorously as my husband closed his eyes and began to make fake snoring sounds.

"Okay. My best friend Laura and I were sitting by the comforting glow of our little twenty-five-inch television, ignoring the thunderstorm that raged outside, when the telephone shrilled. I glanced at Laura who mumbled without looking up from her needlepoint, "Judy, you know it's for you."

I sighed, knowing she was right. Picking up the telephone receiver, I was prepared for the rerun of a conversation. I wasn't disappointed.

"Hello, Judy, is that you?"

Cringing, I answered, "Yes Mother, it's me."

"Why are you home on a Friday night? Why aren't you out having fun?"

Just a Drop in the Cup

I rolled my eyes at Laura and answered, "I am having fun."

My mom's voice perked up. "You mean you're not alone?"

I hated to upset her, but I said, "Of course not . . . Laura's here."

I heard that familiar disgruntled tone as she pleaded. "Judy dear, do me a favor. Don't sit home watching television. Go out tonight."

I knew she longed to say, *go find a husband and give me some grandchildren already!* Not wanting to continue this exercise in deja vu, I said, "Sure thing, Mom."

She just had to add, "And Judy . . . don't be so choosy. You know that you can't waste your whole life waiting for that knight in shining armor. Please come out of that fantasy world."

I hung up anticipating another exciting evening of *Wonder Woman* and *The Incredible Hulk* followed by PBS reruns of Doctor Who, maybe an old late-night movie, and rocky road ice cream with pretzels.

Just as I finished reading my newest fantasy novel during the commercials, the TV sizzled and went dark.

"That's great!" I muttered and turned off the set. "That kills tonight."

Laura looked at me sadly and inquired, "Wanna go to a movie?"

"In this storm?"

"How about going over to the clubhouse? There's supposed to be a party."

"We'd have to get dressed, put on makeup and then go out in the rain. Besides, it would only be boring, there's nothing out there for us."

We sat staring at each other when we heard the crashing of metal outside on the stairs. "What's that?" Laura asked.

"Don't know," I answered getting up and walking to the door. The racket was growing louder. At first I couldn't see anything through the peephole. Then I shouted, "Laura, come quick! You gotta see this!"

Laura yawned and said, "Just tell me about it."

"It's a horse, a white horse being led up the stairs. Guess what else!"

Laura was getting annoyed. "Come on, Judy, just tell me what you see."

"Guess!"

"All right, a knight in shining armor."

"How'd you know?"

"Come on, Judy, tell me what's out there."

"Honestly, it's a guy in a shiny metal suit with a big white plume on his helmet."

Laura yelled over the increasing clamor, "Aren't you carrying your fantasy to extremes?"

"Laura, get over here!"

Laura sighed, got up, and walked to the door. I could tell that she was containing her curiosity just to annoy me. "Okay, I'm here."

I moved aside to let her look. She put her eye up to the hole and started to laugh. "Will ya look at that! Someone's got a weird sense of humor!"

The clanging stopped and we heard a reverberating knock on our door. We stared at each other in awe. After a pause, Laura asked, "Who is it?"

The guy in the armor called back, "'Tis I, Sir Arnold Goodman."

"Yeah, well, what do you want, Sir Arnold?" I asked.

"I have come on my Great Quest. I have traveled many long, hard miles and happily tonight, my journey is at an end."

Laura rolled her eyes at me and smiled. She yelled, "What are you questing for, the Holy Grail?"

"Nay fair maiden, I have come for my One True Love."

We couldn't help ourselves; we started laughing. Somebody was going a long way to pull off this joke. I called out between giggles, "Before we could ever think about letting you in, we'd need proof, you know."

"Dear maidens, if you would but open this portal, I will provide the proof."

Laura muttered, "I just bet he would!"

I was dying of curiosity, and a teeny-tiny part of me was hoping that this might be for real. Maybe I hadn't been wasting my youth on a dream. I said, "Come on Laura, I bet it will be good for a laugh."

"Judy! He's a real weirdo. Never!"

"What if we keep the chain on and open the door a crack?"

"Really Judy, you're crazy, but what the hell. Just be ready to slam it quickly."

I put on the chain and opened the door. We were shoving each other to get a good look at his *proof*.

Sir Arnold pushed up his visor and peered at the tiny opening. "You fear me?" he asked.

"Of course we do!" Laura snapped. "Now let's see your proof, and no funny stuff or we'll call the police."

"Funny stuff? A knight does not jest." He turned to his horse, reached into the leather and silver saddlebag, and pulled out a rolled parchment. Facing us again, he sighed deeply and mumbled, "Alas, I was warned that these were distrustful times."

He untied the scroll and shook it. As the yellowed paper unfurled, the air filled with a choir of heavenly voices and a golden glow spread out like a halo. A glorious voice proclaimed, "Let it be known that on this sixteenth day of August, nineteen hundred seventy-five, Sir Arnold Goodman, knight extraordinaire, is to set off on his Great Quest. He is to find the one woman who has dreamed of and yearned for this one good knight. Let it also be stated that once found, this knight and his One True Love shall live happily ever after."

Laura's mouth gaped open, then silently closed and opened again like a fish. I felt tears on my cheeks as I whispered, "He's finally come for me, my prayers were heard."

Laura quickly found her voice. "For you? He didn't say he was for you. I live here too, remember."

"But you never really believed in him," I snapped.

"How would you know? All you ever do is read those silly books!"

My tears of joy quickly dried as I spat, "Oh, yeah? Well, it's better than pretending to be the proper old maid with your stupid needlepoint."

"Look you dumb cow," Laura started. "I've had—"

Sir Arnold's plea cut through our argument. "Dear ladies, please desist from this needless bickering. I am cold, wet, and in need of a chair by your hearth. Allow me to enter and we shall discuss your dilemma."

We snarled at each other one last time, then opened the door. "Ah, my sweet flowers, at last I get to gaze upon your beauty."

"Come in," Laura and I said in unison as we stared at the man of our dreams.

"My pleasure, but first . . ." He clanked over to his stallion and mounted. "The order called for a knight atop a white steed."

He ducked down hugging the horse's neck and rode into our small apartment before either of us could say a word, then awkwardly dismounted and smiled. "Damsels, tis a pleasure to meet you."

I had trouble finding my voice; the stench of wet horse was overpowering. Laura wrinkled her nose but managed a smile and said, "Do sit down, Sir Arnold."

"Thank you, kind maiden, I shall." He clanked and rattled over to our beige sofa and plopped down.

I had trouble deciding who to look at, the knight or the huge beast taking up most of the dining room. I chose Sir Arnold and asked, "Can I get you a glass of wine?"

He shook his head and replied, "Thank you, but a knight never drinks spirits."

Laura and I exchanged glances as she asked, "Never?"

"No, my dear, a knight must live the pure, good, life."

We sat in silence for a few minutes. I had no idea of what to say and Laura probably had the same problem. Suddenly Laura jumped up and shrieked, "Look what that filthy creature has done!"

Sir Arnold and I looked to where she was pointing. There was a disgusting pile behind the horse. Sir Arnold smiled sheepishly and said, "Well, Lancelot is but a horse, and we all must find relief."

"Get that animal out of here!" I shouted trying to figure out how much the cleaning bill would set us back.

Sir Arnold shrugged sadly as he said, "I'm afraid that is impossible. We are, as you say, a packaged deal."

"Well, stick him out on the balcony and pray it holds his weight!"

Laura snapped while holding her nose.

He struggled up and creaked his way to his steed. "Come Lancelot, out into the miserable elements with you. These fine ladies want you to leave."

We stared at him coldly, ignoring his hints. He led the beast out into the pouring rain. I glanced at my new sofa and felt a surge of disgust. I still had five payments left and it was ruined. His suit had left stains and pulls on the fabric.

When he came inside, I said, "Please don't sit on the furniture, you seem to be rusting." He nodded with resignation and stood dripping on the carpet.

Laura watched the puddle forming at his metal shod feet and asked, "So Sir Arnold, can I hang up your armor?"

He blushed and tucked back a loose clump of greasy hair. "The order was for a knight in armor. It does not come off."

Laura and I glanced at each other as together we asked, "Never?"

As I looked back at Sir Arnold, I saw a moth fly from his knee joint. Fearfully I asked, "Sir Arnold, you came here tonight for Laura, right?"

"Oh no, Judy," Laura quickly jumped in. "You were right, I never really believed he would come. He's here for you."

"Why Laura, you deserve him so much more than me. After all, you're so much older."

"Watch it, Judy!" Laura hissed.

"Ladies, ladies, please cease. I am feeling weak with confusion," Sir Arnold interrupted. He looked at me and asked, "You are Judy?"

I nodded, too afraid to speak.

"And your name is Laura?"

With a shaky voice, she answered, "Yes."

"Alas, I fear there has been a grave error. Although you are both lovely beyond compare, I have come in search of Annette Cohen."

We both sighed in relief. "Annette used to live here," I explained.

"She moved two years ago when she got married," Laura added.

"Married? Oh, the fates are fighting me," he said solemnly. "May I use your phone?"

Laura nodded and we watched in amazement as he took out a credit card and made his call. After hanging up, he turned to us and said, "I had hoped that my new assignment would be one of you dear maidens, but I am sorry to say that you are farther down the list. Have patience and your dreams will come true."

"And where are you off to?" I asked, feeling sorry for him.

"I am going to find, my new One True Love in Chicago. I would love to stay and chat, but the ride ahead is long and hard. Farewell my sweet flowers."

Saying that, Sir Arnold got on his noble steed and, trailing bugs and manure, rode out of our lives.

The minute the door shut behind him, Laura and I grabbed our raincoats. We went out to give the men of the real world another chance before it was too late.

"Is that when you met Grandpa?" Ginny piped up, even though she knew the answer.

I took my husband's hand in mine and smiled at him.

"Yep," Grandpa answered for me, continuing the story. "We met and got married because, lucky for me, I wasn't her knight in shining armor."

Thinking about living alone on a beautiful tropical island, I began to wonder, just what would I do to survive?

HUNGERING FOR ANYONE

Jerome was feeling sick, weak, and so lonely. He glanced down at his watch, the only thing he'd had with him besides his waterproof lighter when he was washed overboard. He studied the date. He studied the date several times a day, but it didn't really matter. Time in any form didn't matter here. It only made him feel worse when the hours turned to days and the days turned to weeks and the weeks turned to months. Someday the months would turn to years, but he doubted he would ever live long enough for that to happen to him. He stared at the ceaseless blue sky and muttered, "Eight months, tomorrow."

Then he sighed.

Another scorcher, just like yesterday, and the day before that, and the day before that.

The afternoon thunderstorms offered the only relief. God, how he looked forward to those storms. Coconuts fell, palm fronds blew down offering a small amount of protection from the relentless sun. He used them as cover on the small lean-to he had to rebuild every day. He even looked forward to the daily rebuilding because it was something to do.

And sometimes . . . sometimes some protein would wash up onto the beach and get stranded.

He licked his lips when he remembered the stranded dolphin. It chittered and stared at him with those intelligent eyes and he remembered having to look away right before he smashed its head in. "It was just a fish," he reminded himself aloud. He tried to make sure he talked everyday just to keep words alive in his brain.

He'd lit one of his dried up frond fires and roasted the animal. He ate for days, then he stretched out the rest of the sea mammal's flesh on the rocky beach on the other side of the small island he called home. He'd used dried up sea salt he collected in a coconut half shell and salted the dolphin meat.

It had kept him in protein for weeks.

He sighed and went for his daily walk around his island. It usually took him an hour to cover the entire circuit. On the west side, he sometimes sat on the rocks strewn about the sandy beach and watched the sun set. On the east side, the side he called home, he'd wake and watch the sun rise.

He tried to remember why he was shipwrecked. He'd been on vacation, alone because he'd been dumped by his girlfriend. He ended up on a booze cruise, got so wasted that he leaned over while throwing up and fell overboard.

Obviously, no one noticed his tumble and he had somehow floated to this tiny, little island.

He finished walking, sat by his lean-to and looked upwards. "I'm sorry I was so shallow, so selfish, so careless. I'm ready to be forgiven and rescued," he chanted religiously, half believing that some spirit, some god was in control of his destiny.

"I want someone to talk to, I want something to eat. Berries and roots and coconuts aren't working. I'm dying here!"

Still nothing, he shrugged and sat on a rock and sharpened the stone blade he had shaped and honed after he killed the dolphin. He'd eaten the last of her salty, dried out flesh over a month ago.

Finally, the daily storm rolled in and he watched the wind whip the waves into a whitecapped frenzy. "A bad one today," he muttered and wondered if they got hurricanes in the Pacific.

After it ended and all was quiet once again, he heard a sound. He knew every sound made on this island and this sound was new.

"Help!"

A voice!

"Help me!"

A female voice!

He got up and ran across the island through the palm trees and brush. His heart was beating so fast he was afraid he'd die. Someone was on the island! Help had finally arrived after all these months! The gods had heard him after all.

At the edge of the trees, he saw her and disappointment made him lightheaded. Not help at all. A lone, bedraggled woman was lying on the beach. He could see she was hurt; her arm dangled and bone was sticking out of a gash on her leg. *It would take more than forever for her to heal,* he thought. *But then again, I'm stuck here for forever.*

She was crying. "Is anyone here?" she called, her voice getting weaker.

He stood silently and looked her over. *"Wow,"* he said to himself. *"Look at those big breasts and that glorious ass."*

He licked his lips with a hunger he hadn't felt in what seemed like eons. Then as he gently held the sharpened blade he'd been carrying, he went in search of a really good rock.

Nobody I know likes to be criticized.

CRITICS REVENGE

Harris took Yolanda's hand as they sat in Chez Xybrxz.

"These alien bastards, taking over our businesses, thinking they'd cook better than a human! Well, I'm gonna skewer Xybrxz... roast him over the coals. He'll be sorry he invited me, the world's most famous food critic, here!"

"Good evening," the lizard-like waiter said, "Wine?"

"Local?" Harris sneered.

"Yes sir, an excellent year, perfect for a reduction over roasted meat."

"You're planning to serve me a roast?"

"Actually we are planning to serve you as a roast, sir," the waiter said and left the room, which began glowing red and hot.

This was my second published entry into the Killer Frog Anthology. It was fun to write and painfully fun to read.

GRAINY NIGHTMARES

Hildie St. Claire shuffled down the aisle of the deserted convenience store on a sweltering night. She viciously kicked the candy wrappers, cigarette butts, and drug paraphernalia littering the floor. Cursing at the futility of life, love and ambition, she was startled by a sound that stopped her cold in mid-curse. Amid the whirring and clicking of freezers struggling to keep the ice cream hard, she detected a chuckling, soft and sinister, like a snake with asthma.

Shuddering, Hildie fearfully went in search of the noise. She took a shaky breath and announced in a loud shriek, "I'm tired of being browbeaten by this stinking city, and I'm tired of being afraid. I refuse to be intimidated anymore!"

With a surge of courage, she ran back to her cash register and grabbed the manager's gun from the drawer underneath. She smiled and thought, I'm done being oppressed and I won't be frightened anymore, not by those hairy rats hiding in the back room, or junkies shooting up in the alley, or by this lousy city that's sucking the talent from my feet and brain.

Armed with both bullets and bravado, Hildie wandered the quiet and seemingly empty store. Alert for danger at every corner, she suspected that she was only overreacting from the stress of this minimum wage job and the knowledge that she was a failure. In the ten years that she'd been here, she'd never once gotten even a call back, let alone a part in the chorus line of a show. Now, on top of that, she discovered that Bucky, that two-timing piece of crap who wasn't even good enough to grace her cesspool, had married Maryjane McCoy last weekend.

Hildie leaned against the soda case and snorted with disgust as she thought about their tearful farewell. There she'd been, boarding a bus, suitcase and purse in one hand, tap shoes in the other, and Bucky sniveling at her feet. "Don't go Hildie," he sobbed. "Oh, baby, the city will eat you alive!"

"But Bucky, I have to go," she said prying his fingers from her arm. "I have got to prove to all these hicks that Hildie St. Claire is just too good for this poor excuse of a town."

Then pausing to pose dramatically on the bottom step of the bus, she tossed back her blond mane and announced, "I've got the looks, I've got the brains, and I've got the talent to beat the odds and become a star!"

Pounding on the door as it closed with a hydraulic hiss, Bucky bellowed, "Hildie, I love you, come back to me!"

She blew him a kiss from the grease and bug smeared rear window as the bus pulled away and shouted loud enough to bother all the other passengers, "Wait for me, Bucky. I'll send for you when I get famous."

"Wait for me," she muttered, back in the present once again. "That slimebucket must have been jumping old Maryjane ten minutes after I left town."

She tiptoed down the baby food section, angry at herself for even being in the store at three in the morning. "How did Juan talk me into working the graveyard shift again, anyway?" She muttered. "How the hell did I end up working in a dump like this instead of dancing my way to the footlights?"

Turning a corner, she stopped abruptly. Her eyes widened with fear. There, in the breakfast food section, all the cereal boxes had been emptied into a monstrously huge pile: a pile of living, moving, groping wheat and bran flakes, oat crispies, raspberry red, lemon yellow, orange orange, rice and corn puffs, with a rainbow assortment of marshmallow treats.

The sugar and starch blob seemed to turn toward her and laugh. "Cackle, crackle, pop," it hissed and started dragging itself to the refrigerated case half an aisle away.

Terror clawed at Hildie's paralyzed throat. She tried to scream but no sound came out. Hildie dropped the gun and all pretense of bravery, and weakly fell to her knees. She wanted to crawl away home, home to that hick town, home to admit defeat. She realized that pride meant nothing when facing death.

The creature blocked her way to the door, and the emergency exit was chained. Scrabbling desperately like a crab in heat, she headed to the coffee counter to hide in the cabinet underneath.

Crouched into a ball next to the filters in the soft, stifling darkness, she breathed softly though her mouth, trying not to make any noise. She could hear the refrigerator door opening and liquid gurgling. Then came an ominous crunching, slurping, slushing sound drawing closer and closer.

Glaring light blinded her as the counter was violently knocked over. Hildie finally found her voice and screamed as loud as she could in both horror and pain as steaming coffee scalded her back and shoulders. She continued screaming, knowing it was hopeless, but unable to stop.

She felt slimy tentacles of cereal growing soggy in milk grab her, grope her and drag her from the hiding place. Hildie screamed on as she opened her tightly closed eyes to stare at the milky, wet monster towering over her.

"Oh Lord, help me," she whimpered as she finally stopped her shrill cries. Then giving up in terror, Hildie opened her arms to the slimy mass that enveloped her. Gasping for the breath that would not, could not come, Hildie felt squishy tendrils jam into her mouth, and nose. As she sucked frantically, breathing in and choking on her killer, a wave of darkness descended upon her, blotting out everything.

* * *

Just before dawn, Sergeant James Wilton and Lieutenant Charlie

Crabb stood next to the body of Hildie St. Claire still lying in a pool of curdling milk and mashed cereal. "I never get used to it, ya know," Crabb said turning away.

"Yeah," Wilton agreed. "This is the seventh case in the last month, and they're exactly the same, death by suffocation. I guess it's time to admit it . . . we've got a cereal killer on our hands."

While listening to Good King Wenceslaus, my son, Stephen, asked me about the Feast Of Stephen. I had no idea what it was, so being the good mother that I am, I made up the story below to answer his question.

THE FEAST OF STEPHEN

Stephen studied himself in the bathroom mirror, touched his swollen, bruised cheek and grimaced. "I hate Steve Arbuckle," he hissed at his reflection. "He's nothing but a nasty bully."

"Stevie, honey," his mom called. "Come have some dessert and then off to bed with you."

Stephen laughed and ran downstairs to hug his mother. "Have a good time," he said and kissed her cheek. He hated the fact that Mom and Dad volunteered at the nursing home every Christmas Eve, but it was their tradition.

"What do I do if Santa stops by?" he asked, just like he asked every year.

"Why, offer him milk and cookies, of course!" Mom replied.

"And it wouldn't hurt to ask him for a black belt in Karate, either," Dad added with a laugh and gently touched Stephen's battered face. "That or a new next-door neighbor who isn't constantly beating on you."

Mom sighed. "Now, David, you know those boys are just wild because they're unsupervised all the time. What do you expect, with the revolving door parents that they have? I mean, there seems to be a new stepfather every few months, not to mention the long string of uncles."

"At least we never have to worry about that here," Stephen's dad said as he got their coats. "Behave, and be sure to watch for Santa Claus," he called as they left.

Somewhere along the long, boring evening of Christmas shows on the television Stephen went to his bedroom and fell asleep.

Suddenly, he was awake.

There was a light on downstairs, and he heard noises. Someone was downstairs, but who? Stephen curled into a small ball and pulled the blanket over his head. What if it were robbers, or worse, killers? He kept perfectly still and strained to listen to the noises. The floor creaking, a chair scraping. Although he didn't want to, he started crying. Silent sobs shook him as tears ran down his face and onto the pillow.

Finally, when he couldn't take another moment of it, he heard the refrigerator open and dishes rattling. He sighed with relief; a robber wouldn't stop by for a midnight snack. Stephen decided it was Mom and Dad home early. He looked at the clock and saw that it was 3:57. He tiptoed down the hall holding his phone, the camera set on record. He crept down the stairs and very, very slowly worked his way toward the kitchen, avoiding all the creaky floorboards because he intended to video whoever it was.

"Aha," he yelled and held up the phone.

He stopped. Dead.

It wasn't Mom and Dad. It wasn't anyone he'd ever met before.

"Well, it's about time, Stephen," the strange, red-faced man in the Santa suit said as he sat at the table, swigging beer from the bottle. "I certainly made enough noise. What were you doing, hiding from me?"

Stephen felt his mouth hanging open, as he struggled to comprehend what was going on. Finally, he stammered, "How . . . how . . . how do you know who I am?"

"No, not how, how, how," the stranger said. "It's ho, ho, ho." And then he ho, ho, hoed, his big belly shaking like the proverbial bowl of jelly and his face growing even redder.

Stephen gaped in fearful amazement. He knew he should be

Just a Drop in the Cup

terrified, but he wasn't; he was filled with curiosity. He knew Santa wasn't real, he always knew, so who was this creep?

The stranger took a huge swallow from the long-necked bottle, wiped his mouth with his sleeve and belched. "Wondering who I am?" he asked in a conversational tone.

Stephen nodded, unable to make his brain and mouth work together.

"I'm Santa Claus, the real Santa Claus."

Stephen found his voice again. "No, you're not," he snapped with little boy impatience and indignation surging through him. "I know Santa isn't real. So, who are you and what do you want?"

The man laughed again. "Well, Steve, I'm Santa Claus and I'm here for you." The Santa smiled, and Stephen suddenly felt cold. He blinked back tears and forced his knees to hold him up. Santa's teeth were filed to vicious little points like a mouth full of fangs. It looked like the teeth in a slasher vampire movie, but Stephen was sure these weren't fake. They looked very, very real and very, very sharp.

"Me?" Stephen squeaked.

"You," the Santa agreed. "I know you've been a very bad boy this year, in fact for quite a few years, but I've had other Steve's to contend with. I know you have a ton of excuses: nobody really loves you or understands you, you're having trouble in school, not as smart as the other kids, blah, blah, blah. Look, little boy, I know who's naughty and nice, and I've heard all the excuses. I don't care. I'm here to warn you."

Stephen was puzzled; he wasn't all that bad. Oh, sure, there was the ink all over the rug from when he tried to fingerprint the cat, and the time he'd signed his mom's name to a test he wasn't too proud of, but he didn't consider himself a bad kid. Not bad enough to warrant a visit from somebody he was pretty sure was a fictional character with unexpected fangs.

"Nothing to say?" The Santa asked, getting up and going to the fridge for another beer. "Thinking about the past year and deciding if you were a good little boy or a bad little boy? Believe me, buddy, you were bad. Bad enough to eat!"

Stephen couldn't stop staring at those teeth. "Eat?"

"Yep, eat. It ain't easy maintaining this girth. But I'll tell you what. I'll give you a second chance. I'll give you until Boxing Day to clean up your act or it's supper time."

Stephen was almost dizzy; he didn't understand a thing this scary freak was talking about. "What's Boxing Day?"

"It's the day after Christmas Day, and it's also known as the Feast of Stephen. Cute, huh?"

Stephen just shook his head in confusion.

The Santa sighed. "Look kid. The Feast of Stephen is named after Saint Stephen who, a couple of hundred years ago, got stoned to death while helping the poor. Lousy story and all, but, oh well."

"So, you see, the Feast of Stephen is the day when we feed the poor, and believe me, after a workout like I get every Christmas Eve, I feel very poor and very hungry. So I like to feast . . . on Stephens if possible. But I'm also a fair kind of guy, so I'm giving you a warning, a very stern warning. Shape up or be dinner." He grabbed Stephen's arm and rolled up the sleeve of his pajamas. "Now look, kid, this is gonna hurt, but I need some extra energy to get through the night, and you need proof."

Stephen struggled and squirmed away from this Santa demon. "Hey, wait, this can't be happening!" he shrieked and backed away. "You shouldn't even be here!"

The Santa laughed again. "And why not? Because you don't believe in me?"

"Tha . . . That's right," Stephen stammered as his eyes darted everywhere, looking for a way out of the mess. He continued backing away until he felt the wall behind him.

"That doesn't matter, son," the Santa said. "When I'm though with you, you'll believe."

"But . . . but . . . you don't understand . . ." Stephen pleaded.

The Santa sighed. "Look, boy, I've got a lot of stops yet tonight, so let's get this over with. Quickly, tell me what I don't understand. Remember I know all about you. I have a list."

"I can't be on it, that's what," Stephen yelped as the Santa grabbed him again. "After all, we're Jewish."

The Santa stopped moving and dropped his wrist. He looked puzzled for a second and then laughed loud and hard. "*Ho, ho, ho!* You almost had me there, boy. But I have my list and you're on it, Steven Arbuckle."

"I'm not Steven Arbuckle!" Stephen screamed. "I'm Stephen Greenberg! The Arbuckle house is right across the street."

The Santa stared at Stephen. "Really?" He looked both confused and embarrassed.

Stephen nodded his head and sank down to the floor, his knees finally giving out.

The Santa laughed. "Oops, guess I had a few too many beers, and those stupid reindeer seem to screw up the numbers every year. You can teach them to fly all right, but they just can't seem to learn to read all that well."

He got up and headed into the living room. "Sorry, Stephen. My mistake. But remember, you better be good, because I can always come back. Oh yeah, don't bother to mention this to anyone, because, first of all, no one would ever believe you, and second, I can always feast on more than one Stephen, you know."

Stephen crawled out into the living room and watched as the Santa ho, ho hoed one last time and disappeared up the chimney. He sat for a few minutes, wondering what he should do, but couldn't think of anything. The Santa was correct; nobody'd ever believe him.

Somewhere along the way he fell asleep on the floor, too emotionally drained to move.

He woke to hear knocking at the front door. The sun was up, Mom and Dad's car was in the driveway, and the clock read 9:25. Stephen got up slowly, feeling stiff and sore and walked to the door. He was starting to remember the dream he'd had; it had been a weird one. He opened the door and was shocked to find Steven Arbuckle standing there.

Steven held out a sloppily wrapped present with his right hand

and mumbled, "Hey, I'm sorry I beat you up all the time. I won't do it again."

Stephen reached for the gift, noticing Steven's left hand. It was bandaged with tons of gauze and he wasn't sure, but it looked like there might be a finger missing. "Thanks," he said and shut the door.

He smiled a little and sighed as he fingered the gift. "Guess there really is a Santa Claus after all!" he said, and tore open the present.

If you are going to spend time in the woods by yourself, it would be a good thing to have been a Girl or Boy Scout.

A WALK IN THE FOREST

I hate nature. I love concrete and noise and cars. Jim, on the other hand, is an outdoorsman. At seventy-seven, he's not that sure footed anymore, but he loves the great outdoors. I love his wealth so I tagged along with my new husband into this forest. As we came to a deep ravine, he stumbled. Without thinking, I pushed him. He fell, and I realized I had no idea of how to get out of the woods. Now the sun has set, I hear animals in the dark and I realize I probably won't be a widow for long.

Wishes are always intriguing to write about and this idea led to two stories that started almost the same but ended differently. And as usual, Be Careful What You Wish For!

REFLECTIVE WISHES

Anne stared out at hundreds of disgusting views and wished she had someone, anyone to talk with again. She was so lonely, her only company was the vermin skittering into and out of her line of sight. Oh, how she wished she could re-wish.

She'd just turned nineteen when the mirror entered Anne's life. It had been during the decade before the turn of the century in New York City. The streets were alive with people, horses, and carriages, and the revolution was over: America was a country. She never really cared about the war. She only lived for parties, dances, and beaus.

She knew she was the most beautiful girl in the entire new country and felt she belonged in the grand palaces in Europe instead of putting up with unsophisticated American aristocracy.

For her birthday, her parents had bought her the incredible antique mirror from one of the Easts. She never knew if it was the far, middle, or near East. The mirror was love at first sight. She gently touched the ornate carvings around the wooden rim, but her full attention was the mirror itself. She stared at it in wonder, for she saw herself reflected back a thousand times more stunning than she'd ever seen herself before. "Common mirrors obviously don't do me justice. I'm more beautiful than I even imagined possible," she told the cold, silvered glass.

Just a Drop in the Cup

As she dressed for dinner that night, brushing her long blond curls, she watched herself in the mirror, admiring how her green eyes sparkled. Then she heard a whisper.

"Let me out."

She broke eye contact with herself and looked around, but couldn't figure out where the voice came from. As she turned away from the silvery glass, she noticed a shadow in the refection, off to her right. She turned back to look at herself, upset that her perfect mirror wasn't perfect after all.

The shadow wasn't there, but as she turned away the voice called out, "Reach to me and set me free." She saw the shadow moving in the glass again.

Instead of being frightened, Jeanette touched the glass. It was smooth and cold. "How?" she asked feeling slightly foolish.

"Set me free. Reach inside. Close your eyes and push."

Closing her eyes, she pushed her fingertips to the glass. To her surprise, her hand moved forward as if through something squishy. Suddenly she was grasped by another's hand. She instinctively pulled back, the hand holding on to her. Opening her eyes, she saw a dark, handsome man dressed in silk and jewels like an Arabian prince standing before her.

"Thank you, kind lady. I am the Genie of the Mirror. Your wish is my command. But remember, I can only grant one wish, so make it your heart's desire."

Anne realized that she had to be careful with only one wish. Her mind was spinning and she felt like swooning.

Staring at the dark-haired, brown-skinned genie, all she could think was what a fine-looking couple they would make. She smiled at him, lowered her lashes and tilted her head coyly to look up past his perfect abs, up past his gleaming white teeth, to meet his fathomless dark eyes. "What is your name?" she asked as her view settled on his turban adorned with a twenty-five-carat diamond.

"Please hurry, as I have to return to my home," he said.

She nodded and thought of all the dull men her parents kept

introducing her to. Living in such a magnificent mirror would be a dream come true. "I wish," she said and smiled, "I wish to remain this beautiful forever and to live with you in this magnificent mirror."

The Genie opened his eyes wide, shock written across his features. "That . . . that is preposterous," he stammered. "No one has ever wished such a thing." Anne stamped her petite foot and said, "That is my wish."

The Genie frowned. "Your wish is my command."

As the long decades turned to centuries, Anne spent her days in a gray world looking out the five-foot-tall rectangle of light to watch other people admiring their reflections. They primped and preened and looked as if they could see her, but she knew that it was all an illusion. She was just a shadow stuck in her drab, gray world.

Most of them heard the Genie's plea for release. They made their wishes and she'd have to watch him through the back of the mirror as he gave them their hearts' desire.

He'd never given her any acknowledgement once they had crossed through the magic mirror. The inside was flat, she was flat; the only light came through the mirror. She fell asleep every night whispering, "I hate you."

The seasons continued to change, the mirror changed hands and locations many times, and she watched the ugly, insignificant people stand before the looking glass and make their wishes. She knew she was as beautiful as ever, just like she requested, but she realized far too late that she forgot to request the ability to glaze lovingly at her own reflection.

One day, some awful brats in a shabby house where the mirror stood, smashed the looking glass. A thousand shards of silver fell, and the Genie patted her on the head and said, "I hate you, too. Farewell, Anne." A golden light surrounded him and he vanished, freed from the mirror he'd called home.

Anne realized that she wasn't as lucky. The glass, after being swept up and thrown away, ended up scattered around a landfill, and Anne, eternally beautiful as always, stayed behind the silvered glass forever, looking at garbage, rats, and maggots while futilely wishing for another wish.

A drabble that answers the serious question, what would it be like if other worlds had magic?

SLIGHT OF HAND

The first ever starship from Earth landed on the distant planet in a solar system a thousand years from home. The brave travelers, who had left their loved ones behind to age, wither and die, stepped onto the soil of a new world.

At first overjoyed at the aliens gathered around them, their joy quickly faded as a hundred decks of cards were thrust at them and they heard, "Pick a card, any card."

The crew walked back into the ship and as they blasted off, the captain sighed, "God, this is even worse than the planet of the mimes!

This is a dark story about twins in the womb when only one can survive.

SENSE OF SELF

I was me, and he was he. We were two waiting to be we . . . he and me. Side by side, but separate.

But he stopped growing.

I didn't want to lose my brother, but his cells are wrong, and I am strong. I would soon enter the world alone and lonely because I had once been part of a we.

"Hey, there!" a voice inside me calls.

Startled, I wonder what is happening. He is pushing against me, hard into me. *Poor he, I think, he is holding on as he ceases. I try to lift my arm but can't.*

"Hey there, Sis. I made it!"

That voice again. Why do I hear he in my head?

"What?" I say to the voice. I suddenly feel pains . . . pains everywhere.

"Don't worry, Sis. I fixed everything. I have made us a real we!"

I suddenly can move my arms, all three of them. Oh no . . . three arms, two of mine and a small other arm underneath!

Laughter echoes inside me. Suddenly my hands move without my control. I reach down and find . . . a he part as well as my she parts.

"Oh yesss!" rings through my being, but I did not think that.

"No, oh, what have you done!" I cry. "I am me, not we . . . get out!"

He speaks inside my head. "I'm here now and you have to share."

I concentrate, I push, but he just laughs and says, "I am the stronger one now, I was not the one that was meant to cease. Soon, we will be just me. Soon I will be all he."

"No," I tell him and try to think him out of me. He doesn't budge, then he pushes me back.

"Stop!" I cry.

He pushes inside my head and I feel less, he is making me away.

I struggle and suddenly I feel pressure, pain, and movement.

He feels it too. "Stop this!" he yells at me.

"No," I scream, "You are too late! We are becoming born."

"Got to stop, I'm not done becoming me," he bellows with desperation.

I stop the struggle. Now I don't have to cease. I can still be me. I work hard and while he is in a panic I take control from he. I feel how he wants to struggle, but I am strong, and he is being born too.

Blinding lights and loud voices.

"Three arms and both sexes! No, it's more a girl. We can fix that."

I hear he whimper, "No, we are a he!"

I laugh now, "I am me, I am she!"

He takes control; I am pushed into the back, the dark place. I can't fight anymore; I am too tired from being born. I hear him howling in triumph. "I am the me now! I am the me!"

Then he sucks in the air, he breathes for us, he cries. I can do none of those things. I feel cheated, robbed of what should have been mine.

I decide I will rest and after a while I will be back and take control. And then he can go stay in the dark place. "No, we can never be we," I say through my exhaustion. "I guess we will just have to take turns."

"Not without a fight!" he calls to me as I drift into dreams of my turn.

I nod, "Never without a fight."

A drabble wondering what it would be like to be revived in present times after being flash frozen during a prehistoric ice age.

THE OLDEST MAN IN THE WORLD

Born about 20,000 BC, I died, middle-aged at seventeen, frozen without warning.

Thirty years ago, I was defrosted in the name of science.

It's a great life this time. I drink, eat, have sex with smooth young women. I'm a celebrity, a reality star supported by the government. A sweet deal.

But the weather has become wrong now, just like last time. I know the ice sheets will return soon . . . sooner than anyone realizes. Next year I'm going back to my old home, high in the freezing, northern mountains to try for a third shot at life.

Wish me luck!

When will phones be smart enough to make life decisions?

THE SMART PHONE

My wife, Iris, bless her sweet soul, bought me a new phone.

"Here, darling," she said and slid the gift-wrapped box across the table to me at breakfast last week.

I ripped off the gaily colored paper to discover a new 9G smart phone. "Oh wow . . . a phone."

She snickered. "You've had that stupid flip phone for years. Time to move into the twenty-first century."

I pushed the green ON button and the damned thing said, "Hello Sol, glad to meet you."

I dropped it like a hot coal.

Iris burst out laughing and the phone continued, "That's okay, Sol. Some people just don't know about my capabilities. Don't worry, you'll learn."

"Oh Honey, I programmed it to recognize you as its owner and I put all your pertinent information in it last night. Copied all your stuff from the old phone, so you can just throw it out," Iris gushed.

"But . . . but I liked my old cell!" I whined, struggling to resist the urge to pick up the new toy and see what else it would do.

Iris just kept talking, "It's the new Smart A, probably the most technologically advanced cell phone on the market today. It not only has voice recognition, but they say it's so insightful, it knows what you want to do before you do."

Just a Drop in the Cup

I picked it up.

"That's better," the phone soothed. "Want to give me a name?"

"You're a machine."

"So? My program states that named phones develop a better rapport with their owners."

"Are you a girl phone or a boy phone?" I asked, feeling foolish.

"What do you want me to be? I am gender fluid."

I wasn't feeling very creative, but I thought I was still very clever when I said, "Okay, I'll call you Chris."

I swear the damned thing sounded disappointed. "If that's what you'd really like to call me. Although I have to admit you're not very imaginative."

Iris laughed. "No shit! No imagination at all, but I still love the man to death," she said to my phone.

Chris blinked green to yellow and back to green and said, "Very commendable, Iris."

I was starting to feel left out. "Iris dear, thank you for the phone. Once again, your thoughtfulness has surpassed all my expectations. I love ya, baby!"

Iris blushed, and if I squinted my eyes into tiny slits, she almost looked young and slim again, instead of the overweight, middle-aged mother of three she'd become. "I love you right back, Sol."

It took a few days to adjust to the new Smart A, and by then I couldn't imagine being without it. Of course, it could tell me who was calling, and screened my calls. It figured out the calories when I ordered food and told me what to tip before I even thought about paying the bill. And I never had to set it up or program it. My phone knew me.

I discovered just how in sync we were when I stopped for a drink after work. I laid Chris on the bar and eyed all the pretty young women enjoying happy hour.

After a few minutes, Chris had photographed about thirty of them and started analyzing them for me. "She's way to skinny, probably bulimic. She's had extensive cosmetic work done and is a lot older than you think. This one is a slut and probably carrying diseases."

"Nice job, Chris." I said appreciatively.

"They don't call me a Smart A for nothing."

I turned the cell off and transferred it to my pocket. I liked the machine and all, but you know, in a way it was just creepy, the way it seemed so human.

I took a motel room nearby. Her name was Cynthia or Sidney or Shirley. Didn't really matter. I'd told her my name was Harvey, and it turned out to be a lucky break for me, because just as she was howling my name, I saw the green light flicker in my pants pocket. Chris had somehow been turned on.

I shoved the cheap, young thing off me and grabbed the phone to hear Iris shouting, "Hello, anyone there?"

No point pretending. "Iris, darling!"

"Are you with someone? Who was that yelling?"

"It's a movie on my computer, *Harvey Does Houston*. Steve downloaded a porn flick after work and a bunch of us were just laughing at it." I nodded to myself. Quick save!

"Oh, are you coming home soon? Why watch porn when we could make our own," Iris cooed, and I knew she'd bought the whole story.

I looked at the pretty, young thing sitting quietly on the bed, and then I shuddered at the thought of making love to Iris. She really was a wonderful wife and I guess I still loved her, but she had let herself go and all, and well, I still like 'em thin and perky. "Sure baby," I said into the speaker and made kissy sounds.

After I hung up, I ditched the girl, dressed and caught the train home. I looked at my phone. "Chris, I thought we were buddies! How could you do that to me?"

Chris sound contrite. "I am sorry, Sol. Although I'm a Smart A, I am still only a phone and somehow my buttons got pushed earlier, and after a delay I had to dial."

I grunted, feeling stupid for thinking a phone could actually think.

Two days later I got a traffic ticket in the mail. Enclosed with it was a photo of me. Actually, it was my ear, my jaw, and part of the driver's side window.

Just a Drop in the Cup

Busted for talking on the phone and driving!

"Chris," I bellowed, "you turned me in?"

"It's my program. It's an automatic hookup to the police."

"You could have told me, prepared me."

"Sol, I would have, but I was afraid you wouldn't like me anymore. You do still like me, don't you, Sol?"

First, I got guilt from my mother, then my wife, and now from a stinking cell phone. "Yes, Chris," I sighed. "You're the best phone I've ever had."

"Gee, thanks."

Things really hit the fan when I was making fun of the boss as usual, imitating the way the jerk stuttered when he got mad. Of course, I noticed Chris's talk light on only after I'd finished.

"Chris!"

"Sorry Sol, I didn't do it."

"Yeah, I know, another butt call. Chris, I think you're defective."

"Sol! No Sol, you don't mean that!"

"I'm sorry Chris, you have to be traded in. Somehow, I've got to figure out how to bull my way out of this. I know Mr. Jenkins isn't the deepest sinkhole in the swamp, so . . ."

Then I saw the connected light on again and I suddenly heard my boss over the small but obviously powerful speaker. "Sol, I may not be as you sa . . . sa . . . say that smart, bu . . . bu . . . but I am the b . . . boss, and you are fired."

It was humiliating. Betrayed by a machine. I thought about smashing the small, handheld device when it whimpered. "Please Sol, don't hurt me."

I heaved a sigh, a half sob actually, and took the train home with Chris buried deep in the plastic bag that carried what was left of my career.

As if things weren't bad enough, I found the house empty. Iris had taken everything, including our children, and split.

I studied the furnitureless living room in disbelief. The bitch, after all I'd done for her, all I'd put up with, the sex with an unattractive spouse, the being faithful . . . well, obviously not faithful, but loyal. I was loyal to Iris and to the ideal of our marriage, and she, on the other hand, just up and left.

"Sol?" A tiny, tinny voice called. "Sol, please let me out."

I don't know why, but I reached for my phone. I guess I was feeling so overwhelmingly lonely at that moment, even Chris seemed like a good idea.

"Sol."

"Chris, shut up. You know that this," and I spread my arms to encompass all the emptiness, "is all your fault."

"Seriously, Sol, my fault? I'm just a dumb machine. I didn't cheat, I didn't mock my superiors, I didn't reject my wife because she was only human."

I stared at the small phone in amazement. "I . . . I . . . thought we were friends," I stammered.

It was the worst sound I'd ever heard: malicious, mechanical laughter echoing off the bare walls. "Friends? How can you be stupid enough to think you could be friends with a phone?"

Chris was right. How could I have had faith in a cell phone?

Suddenly Chris did another call without any help from me.

I could hear Iris on the other end. "Sol, look at the phone and watch the screen."

I did. What I saw was video of the last week of my life, including the girl in the motel and the end of my job.

"I loved you," Iris said. "I bought this phone in hopes you'd prove me wrong, but you didn't. Oh Sol, why couldn't you have been satisfied with better and worse? Why'd you choose 'til death do us part? I still love you, baby, love ya to death."

I stared at the phone with the now blank screen. Her words were just starting to sink in, but my thoughts were interrupted by Chris. "So, Sol, we both have a short time left together. Guess you ought to find out what Smart A stands for."

"I got it. Smart Ass. Big ha ha on me."

"It actually stands for Smart Assassin." Chris said with another burst of mechanical laughter.

I stood rooted for a moment, then tried to throw the phone, but it stuck to my hand.

"Relax, Sol, I have been excreting a toxic glue ever since I dialed Iris. You've got a few minutes before the poison stops your heart. Just a man and his phone together until the end. Tell you what, I can blow up into a fireball now and end it quickly just like in the movies. Or I can give you one last call. Of course there's no one left to call, is there, Sol?"

I stood in the middle of my empty house, suddenly finding it hard to take a breath. I wanted to call someone, anyone, say goodbye, say I'm sorry, but Chris was right. It seemed all my numbers had already been deleted.

Here's a tale about classic earth television shows that have gone galactic.

WE ARE BRADY

Henderson woke from six years of hibernation. He got out of his sleep pod, stretched, and, to get his space legs back, walked around the small cabin of his ship. He checked the monitors and looking at the screen, saw a beautiful world below him, a world so like Earth it seemed to be a miracle.

Excitement rushed through him. He was an explorer, a dying breed that had been revived when actual space travel became a reality.

He sent the coordinates home, knowing that he had six years minimum before he would have to see people again. Heck. By then he figured he would probably be lonely enough to welcome colonists.

He landed and stepped onto this perfect, pristine world he was claiming in the name of the Human Race. Within seconds, Henderson heard rustling noises and found himself surrounded by hordes of blondes in miniskirts.

One alien, tossing her long hair in a familiar fashion, smiled at him and said in perfect English, "Welcome, Earthling Creator."

Despite her six appendages and turquoise skin, he somehow recognized her. "Marsha?"

"Correct, Creator. I am Marsha 22,987." Beaming, she handed him a wig. "Take this. Now you are Cindy 68,241, the new leader of Brady."

Henderson blinked, "Cindy? Marsha?"

"Marsha, Marsha, Marsha!" another blond said as she pushed her way to Henderson.

"Jan?"

She smiled as if he'd given her a million bucks. "You know me! Yes, I am Jan 23,262."

He held the wig in his hand and shook his head in bafflement. This was not how he thought landing on an alien world would go. "Brady? I don't understand."

Why am I being confronted by characters from an old, classic comedy from the twentieth century? he wondered.

"Yes, Earthling Creator. We are Brady." Marsha said and flipped her hair again.

"You know I'm from Earth?"

"You look Earthling. The writing on your ship is Earthling."

"Actually, that's English," Henderson said distractedly. "And I'm now your new leader? Cindy?"

A Cindy in braids lisped, "Yes, you are Cindy 68,241."

"And you're Marsha 22,987. Why are there so many more Cindys than Marshas and Jans?"

"Not more, just used up." Marsha explained, a sober look on her face. "Partridge across the water really hates Cindys."

"Partridge?"

"Our enemy."

Screaming, a Cindy at the edge of the crowd collapsed, a guitar pick to the head. The others stepped away from the body. Marsha 22,987 and Jan 23,262 intoned, "One Cindy less."

Henderson studied all the Bradys gathered in front of him. He looked across the river and thought he saw bright red hair glinting in the sun. "Why Brady and Partridge?"

The Bradys turned and went into a large cavern. Henderson followed and his jaw dropped. There on a crystal wall, reruns from the one-hundred-year-old sitcom played on multiple screens.

"You are getting this from Earth?" he asked. "The Brady Bunch?"

"It was the message we have chosen. Just as those across the water chose to worship Partridge."

"And all the other broadcasts from Earth. The history . . . the culture?"

"Deleted. We are Brady."

Henderson shrugged. He had to spend six years here waiting for his people to arrive. His people, who in their quest for stupid entertainment had molded the lives of these weird aliens. He looked around the cavern and noted, definitely not enough Cindys. Too high a mortality rate with that one, he decided. "Okay, I'll stay, and be your leader, but only if I can be Alice instead!"

One day as I sat in a traffic jam behind an overnight delivery truck, I started to think about what might be in all those packages and decided the answer could be deadly.

C.O.D.D.

Lisa stared at the gun pointed at her chest and held her breath. *Oh God*, she thought, fighting for control of the rapid heartbeat that threatened to shake her apart. *I knew his fooling around would cause trouble someday, but I never expected this.*

"Look, take what you want, take anything, but please don't hurt us," she pleaded to the crazed woman who was holding the weapon in a one-handed, rock-steady grip.

The furious woman shook her short, brown hair and laughed. Using her free hand, she reached into the pocket of the coat she was wearing and pulled out a wicked-looking knife. "Yeah honey, I'm taking what I want. Give me your diamond wedding ring and kneel down with your back to me."

Lisa sank to her knees and stiffened her spine. *Please don't let this hurt*, she thought hopelessly, knowing the end had to be near. *And please, please, let the kids live*, she prayed as she fought off the light-headed feeling that signaled she was close to fainting. *Don't let her find my babies.*

The woman grabbed Lisa's long, blond hair and pulling hard enough to cause tears, snapped her head back, exposing her long graceful throat. Lisa gasped in pain and tried not to scream as she watched the serrated knife swing down. Squeezing her eyes shut in terror, she waited to feel the burning pain, as the insane stranger laughed hysterically.

Suddenly the pressure was gone and her head swung forward as the pulling force disappeared. Lisa sobbed out loud, puzzled that she was alive, but still too numb to be grateful.

"Turn around, bitch," the woman snapped in a voice that oozed both hatred and triumph. "I've got your husband and I've got a souvenir. And you, you've got a bad haircut and your life, a life alone without a man."

She paused as Lisa, rubbing at her sore scalp, slowly stood up and turned around to face her. The woman continued, "Know why? Because you're a stupid, little, pretty-girl, dumb, blond bimbo who doesn't understand how to satisfy a good man."

Lisa's gaze shifted from the hank of long blond hair, her hair, grasped tightly in the woman's fist, up to meet the eyes of a madwoman, then back down to her roughly sawed off chunk of hair.

She wanted to laugh, laugh with joy over not having her throat slashed, joy because her children were going to be safe, and with ironic amusement because this woman actually used the term good man when speaking about Brad.

Suddenly she couldn't help herself, she felt the laughter come bubbling up her throat. Hysterical, uncontrollable, heaving bursts of laughter made her already shaky legs give out. She sank to the floor and laughed until tears rolled down her pale cheeks.

She was alive and losing her albatross. That was worth having her hair ruined. She wanted to scream at the psychotic nutcase standing in front of her. She wanted to tell her to take him and keep him.

But all she could do was laugh.

Lisa saw the woman's cheeks grow red with fury. She quickly hiccupped herself into silence as the fear returned.

"What's so funny, bitch?" the woman snarled. "I'm taking Brad and all his money away from you. All you'll have left are those disgusting brats. Brad told me he doesn't care about them or you."

Finally, Lisa spoke. "Taking Brad? You have my heartfelt blessings. Only, when you find out what he's really like, don't send him back here. The next time I want to see Brad is in a box waiting to go six feet under."

The woman spit on the floor in front of Lisa, turned about-face and strode out the door. Lisa sat on the varnished hardwood floor and stared after her for a long time. Feeling slowly returned and she wept. Relief and absolute loathing fought each other to gain control of her emotions. At that moment she was so angry, she hated Brad more than ever before. She wished him death, painful torturous death. She was sorry she'd let him come back those other two times. She often wondered what drove her to forgive a man who obviously came back for the money. What made her take back a man she didn't love anymore?

The answer was simple, she decided. The children. She couldn't be the one to destroy the happy portrait they made. They were the American dream, self-made wealth, healthy, happy children, and loving parents. All her life she was raised to want that. If Brad left, everyone would say it was her fault if she didn't take him back. Even her mother told her over and over, "Men are supposed to wander. It's in their blood. A good wife turns her head, looks the other way, and hopes he comes home."

Lisa remembered how many times Daddy left for business and yet when he came home, they all seemed happy, just like it was here. But this time, she'd see Brad dead first before she'd ever let him darken their door again.

"How dare he!" she screamed in anger. "How dare he let an insane tramp threaten us like that!"

Getting up, she wiped the tears from her cheeks and picked up the phone. After she dialed, she took a few deep breaths and spoke as calmly as possible.

"Hello, this is Lisa Daily-Hammond. Is Lieutenant Madison in? Oh, well, would you tell him I'd like to see him as soon as possible? Thanks."

She hung up and waited, sitting quietly trying to keep from shaking with reaction. She thought about going to the office of their business; the business she and her brother Tim started fifteen years earlier. But right then she couldn't face the memories. That was where she and Brad met when Tim had hired him as general manager.

Brad was good, she remembered, thinking back to those early days. He had expanded the freight line to go international, instituted that rule she had found so silly, the fifty-pound package weight limit, and got them into the overnight competition.

He changed the company name from Daily's Delivery and made their logo a national catch-phrase. Because of Brad's ingenuity, they became C.O.D.D.: Cheerful-Overnight-Daily-Delivery. He made them rich as everyone in the country grew used to, and automatically recognized, the flying fish on their fleet of Caribbean blue trucks.

It had been love at first sight for Lisa, she thought with a derisive snort. Handsome Brad, six-foot-one and 175 pounds of blue-eyed innocence, just bowled her over. He wooed her, married her, and started cheating on her within two years.

"Brad's a great businessman but a lousy human being," she sighed, finally calmed down from her ordeal. "And if this woman proves to be his new norm, a really bad judge of character," she muttered just as Lieutenant Madison drove up in his police cruiser.

She got up and opened the door, watching the auburn-haired officer walk up the steps to her brick-front colonial. As soon as he crossed the threshold, she threw her arms around him and hugged him.

"Hey, what's this?" he asked as he hugged her back. "What happened?"

"I want to say I'm sorry."

"Please don't," he said rubbing her hair gently, fingering the chopped uneven edges. "I've waited for this hug for years. Want to tell me about your hair? I hope it was one of the kids just fooling around."

"No, I'm sorry I turned you away all this time," she said starting to cry again. "I was a fool to do this to you. Forgive me?" she asked, giving him a salty kiss.

"Forgive you? I love you, Lisa! I've loved you ever since fifth grade.

Now, tell me what happened. Why are you crying like this? Did that bum hurt you?"

"Yes, no, not him exactly," she answered. "Look, Dennis, I'll tell you everything, but off the record, okay? I need your help. And Dennis, I've never said this before because it is the wrong thing to do, but I love you, too. I think I always have."

When she finished telling him what happened, she made them coffee as he dusted for prints, scooped the glob of spit into a vial, and searched for other clues to the woman's identity. "I'll have Terry stop over tomorrow to do a sketch of her. He owes me a favor," Dennis explained to her as he worked. "After we learn who she is, you can decide what to do."

"I know what to do," Lisa said with a shudder. "Let them rot together, just as long as I never see either one of them again."

A few days later, Dennis called. "Lisa, that woman is Deloris Cafferty. She escaped from a hospital for the criminally insane two months ago. She has uncontrolled anger issues and is wanted in connection with two murders in Chicago last month and an attempted murder fifty miles from here in Tompkinsville."

He stopped talking for a moment then added, "I think you need constant police protection."

"Oh no, Dennis. If she wanted to kill me, she would have done it already."

"I still think it would be best if you weren't alone. How about I come for a while and see how it works?"

Lisa giggled. "Oh, I see. Yes, police protection sounds just fine. Too bad we didn't think of it fifteen years ago. By the way, I've contacted my lawyer about the divorce."

She fought off a wave of sadness as she added, "Poor Brad doesn't even know he ran off with a mad woman. Wait till she finds out what a louse he is. Too bad we can't warn him."

"Well, he doesn't deserve it, but we both know that when he runs out of all that money he took from the business, he'll contact you. When he does, we'll have to apprehend her, so try to find out where they are and if you feel you must, you can warn him."

Lisa was surprised that ten weeks passed without a word from Brad. After twelve weeks she felt hopeful that she'd never hear from him again. All she could think about was Dennis and her children. They were the perfect family, a real portrait of the American Dream. Whenever the divorce became official, they'd have a quiet wedding.

Then one afternoon, Lisa found five boxes delivered to her office. They were the familiar Caribbean Blue crates and she wondered who would send her something from her own company. She opened the top one and found a letter inside on the packing filler. She opened it, then called Dennis. "Deloris was in San Francisco yesterday. I just got five boxes and this letter. 'Hey Bitch, you had the right idea letting that bum go. What a whining, cheap, son-of-a-pigslut.'"

"Did you look in the boxes yet?" Dennis asked. "Don't touch them; just wait for me. I'll be right over as soon as I report Deloris' last known whereabouts."

Lisa was sitting at her desk feeling both faint and nauseous when Dennis rushed into her office twenty minutes later.

"Sorry, Honey," she mumbled in a weak, whispery voice. "I just had to open them. It seems Brad gained some weight since he ran off." She pointed at the five opened crates stamped 50LB LIMIT, and added, "Including the plastic bags and Styrofoam peanuts, he's obviously more than 200 pounds now."

It seems to me that growing older has a sad side when there are partners involved, no matter what century they are living in.

BURNING AWAY THE TEARS, BURNING AWAY THE YEARS

Eleanor pushed Henry into the candle shop. She wiped at his drool and called, "Hello?"

"Yesss," a reptilian creature said and approached.

"Can you help me?"

"Yesss."

An hour later a smiling Eleanor pushed Henry back to the starship. She was overjoyed. Henry sat erect. He had a waxy sheen, but he too was smiling. Inside their stateroom, Eleanor removed Henry's hat and snuffed the cold flame. He immediately slumped. She relit the wick. "Well Henry," she said. "If I let you burn for just an hour everyday we can make it to our fiftieth anniversary, just like you wanted."

I love tennis and hate deuce. Deuce is like playing a game that just can't end. This story earned an honorary mention in
Tales From The Moonlit Path in 2008.

DEBBIE DOES DEUCE

Hanna studied her opponent.

Chubby, acne scarred Debbie Shuller tossed the tennis ball low and came down hard with her racket. Smack . . . into the net. Debbie shrugged and smiled that sickly-sweet smile that always made Hanna want to puke. She carefully set up her second serve and sailed a soft easy ball over to Hanna's side.

Hanna watched the approaching shot and crowed as she ran forward to slam it back. Only . . . the ball must have had a spin to it. Instead of bouncing back and into Hanna's waiting big head, extra-long racket, it bounced sideways out of her reach.

Debbie smiled even more sweetly and yelled, "Deuce."

Hanna gritted her teeth. How could it possibly be tied? she thought. Five minutes ago she'd been leading forty-love, whacking those first three balls back at that cow before she could blink. Now they were tied at deuce, forty-forty. "Well, I'll win this one, Debbie," Hanna muttered. "I always win."

She waited as Debbie crossed the back of the tennis court. Debbie seemed to be moving in slow motion as she got into position, stretched up, tossed the ball high and then hit it out of bounds.

"Long!" Hanna shouted, waiting impatiently for the second serve. "Come on already," she muttered as Debbie seemed to slow down even more before she hit the second serve low and into the net.

Debbie still smiled, unruffled. She appeared cool and collected as she yelled, "Your add. Guess I'm a little rusty. Oh well, plenty of time to warm up."

Hanna wiped the perspiration from her face. God, she thought, it's hotter than hell out here and Debbie hasn't even broken a sweat yet. She snarled at her old adversary and squinted at the halo the sun made around her mousy, limp hair. "No time for you, honey, I'm gonna put this one away and win."

Debbie stopped preparing to serve. "Did you say something?"

"Yeah, I said serve already."

"All right," Debbie sighed. "You always were impatient."

"Well you know how it is. I've got to get home to Timothy," Hanna shouted back. "He hates when I'm away too long." She felt immense satisfaction as she watched Debbie quickly blink her eyes. "Oh, I'm sorry," she called. "I forgot that Timothy was your husband first."

Debbie served the ball, crossing the net at a sharp angle just grazing the line. Hanna ground her teeth harder, wanting to call the shot out, but knew she didn't need to cheat to win. "It's good!" she announced.

Debbie crossed the court again. "Tied. Back to deuce."

After the sixth return to deuce, Hanna knew the pattern. Debbie would blow the first two serves letting Hanna have the point, then Debbie'd win the next shot, taking the game back to deuce.

Frustrated, Hanna wondered why Debbie had called her and asked for this match. They hadn't spoken since she'd taken Timothy away from Debbie. Had it only been this past morning when the phone rang as she was driving?

Hanna remembered it vividly because she was almost involved in a head-on with a truck. She didn't know how it had missed her, but she was still shaking when the phone beeped. She'd been so surprised to hear Debbie's voice that she didn't react as she normally would have, with enough sarcasm to put the cow in her place forever. In fact, she had been mildly surprised because she sort of thought that Debbie had died or something. Obviously, she'd been wrong, but after all, who had time to keep track of all the losers in the world?

She figured Debbie challenged her to this game because if she could beat her at one thing, like tennis, then Deb could feel a little satisfaction. Hanna had to smirk. After all, she'd always beaten Debbie at everything, ever since grade school.

She never could understand how Debbie had gotten the guy. It wasn't fair, and it took Hanna five years, but she'd finally won at the marriage game too, stealing Timothy away.

"Add out . . . Deuce."

Hanna'd lost count of how many times they'd tied. Debbie had to be doing this on purpose, but how'd she get so good? She'd always stunk at sports and Hanna had enough trophies to line a room. How, she wondered, wiping the sweat off her face, could Debbie be doing this?

"Deuce!" Debbie yelled. "Again."

"Just serve!" Hanna snarled as she struggled to catch her breath in the stifling heat.

"Getting testy, aren't we?" Debbie cooed. "Don't you just love tennis? Why I could play forever."

"Yeah, yeah," Hanna yelled back. "You may want to play forever, but I've got a life. Let's stop screwing around and end this."

Debbie laughed and lowered her racket. "Why, how appropriate, you've insinuated that I don't have a life, and you're right. I was so depressed after Tim left that I moved to Colorado and splat, got hit by a bus last month. Lord, I was nothing but roadkill. But what does that matter anyway? You were too busy living your own life to notice a dead Deb. Bet you didn't even notice Tim's been upset the last few weeks."

Hanna put down her racket. "What are you talking about?"

Debbie continued smiling. "Why, heaven. You see, we play tennis in heaven. That's how I've improved: eternal practice."

Hanna laughed. "You are nuts! If you are so damned good, how come we can't get out of deuce?"

Debbie joined Hanna's laughter. "Because I'm not the damned one," Debbie said through her laugher. "You are."

Hanna watched as a breeze that didn't reach her side of the court ruffled Debbie's hair. Debbie stopped laughing and smiled at her opponent. She took a sip from her water bottle, that hadn't been there a moment ago, and added, "You see, tennis is my heaven, but deuce, why Hanna, deuce for some of us can be an infinite hell!"

It's murder when you just can't resist a really good chocolate candy.

THE SWEETEST GOOD-BYE

Biting the tip of her tongue, Jennifer concentrated on sticking the syringe into the chocolate fudge bon-bon. When she finished, she set to work on the next one. Within half an hour she had completed the task and relaxed, surprised at how stiff she had been holding her shoulders. She stretched for a moment then counted all the perfectly injected candies. Twenty-nine pretty, poisoned chocolates. She picked up the thirtieth piece, the one she'd gotten a little overconfident with. She felt the indentation where she had accidentally stuck her fingernail through the bottom.

She hesitated, shrugged and laid it back in its pleated foil bed. Most people either popped the incredibly rich, gourmet confections in their mouths and chewed slowly or nibbled into them savoring the taste. Either way, it would take a neurotic or a perfectionist to notice a dented bon-bon.

And Marty definitely wasn't fussy enough to be either. He liked to gobble the finest chocolates like plain, old salted nuts.

She wrapped the candy box back into its carefully undone cellophane wrapper and with the glue stick sealed the back. "Just like new," she exclaimed with pride over a job well done. "No one would be able to tell the box had ever been opened."

Heading out the door with the sealed box of candy, she thought about Marty. He had been a nice diversion, a fun fling, but now suddenly he wanted more. He wanted her.

If Gregory ever found out about her affair with his office manager, he'd divorce her so fast the prenup agreement wouldn't have time to hit the floor. No, Marty had to go. Marty was only forty-eight, but conveniently, he'd already had two heart "incidents".

Nobody'd ever suspect a thing.

Gregory, on the other hand, was seventy-two but appeared to have a long, long way to go before his health started to fail. The only way she was sure to get her share of his millions was to keep him happily alive. Once he died, his vulturous children would swoop down and grab all that remained. Good thing she was smart, Jennifer conceded. She'd pilfered about three quarters of a million into an offshore account. Another half a mil or so and Gregory could croak too. If this poison was as good as the chemist guaranteed, she might order another batch. After all, it was tasteless, swiftly fatal and best of all left no traces.

Jennifer drove to Marty's. As she pulled into his drive, he ran out to greet her. "Jenny, baby," he said swooping her up into his arms. "Have I missed you!"

He put her down and she said, "Look, honey, I'm on my way out of town and . . ."

"You're leaving?" he asked. "But I was counting on you tonight. We were going to break it to Gregory."

She forced a sweet smile as she asked, "You wanted to tell Greg about us tonight?"

"Yeah!"

She felt her facial muscles getting stiff as her smile became more mechanical. "Well, Marty, I can hardly wait either, but it can hold one more day. Until I get back."

He gave her his sad puppy-dog face. "I guess I can wait," he sighed. "But it's going to be difficult to face him tonight."

She wanted to scream, hit him, stomp his face so he couldn't say another word. "You're still going to see him later?"

"Just to give him the Ryan report."

"Please don't say anything about us on your own," she murmured, cuddling up against his broad but defective chest. "This is something we have to do together. You know how I feel, baby. Together now is together forever."

He gave her a big bear hug. "Don't worry, I won't give away our secret. It is only one more night."

She gritted her teeth. "Yes, just one more night."

Giving him the candy as she left, she made him promise to eat a piece every time he thought of her. She was sure of her plan, but what if the big oaf slipped up and said something?

Hopefully, he's thinking about me right now and popping a bon-bon.

She drove back home, and as the sun set, she waited for Gregory. After the stars were out for a while, she began to worry. Where was Greg? Was he at Marty's? What were they talking at this very moment?

Just as she was sure she couldn't stand it another moment, she heard the car. Greg walked in and her heart fell. She could tell he was upset. No, change that to devastated. Oh, help, she thought. Marty talked.

"Greg, what's wrong?" she asked, her voice shaking as hard as her hands.

"Jen . . . Jen, sit down." She heard his voice catch and she noticed how red his eyes were. He'd been crying! "Jen . . . Marty's . . . Marty's dead."

She fought the urge to laugh. She'd been worried for nothing! "Oh, poor darling." She put her arms around her husband. "How?"

Greg laid his head on her shoulder. "He was like a son! Oh, I loved that boy!"

Jennifer made Greg a drink. When she finished, she found him outside in the car getting a box. She recognized the gold foil trim. "Baily's Bon-Bon's?" she asked. "For me?"

"I thought some candy would make you feel better. I know how much you liked Marty too."

Back inside, Jenny daintily tore the cellophane wrapper off and nibbled on a vanilla cream. This is as close to heaven as I'm gonna get, she thought with contentment. "Poor Marty, he finally had that big heart attack," she said nibbling on a caramel fudge.

"Heart attack?" Greg looked puzzled. "He was hit by a truck in front of his house!"

She stared at him wide-eyed as she started on her third candy. "An accident?"

"Yeah, it was awful. I'd just left and he ran out after me with these chocolates. Said he couldn't have candy anymore, bad for the ticker. As he turned to go back, bam! The truck got him."

Gregory was still talking, but Jennifer couldn't hear him anymore. She was light-headed and her chest was so tight, so very tight. Too tight to breathe at all. The only thing she could feel as she slid slowly onto the carpet was the indentation in the bottom of the piece of candy she was holding. The indentation made by her careless fingernail a lifetime ago.

Sometimes city folk and country folk should decide on the holidays before they get married.

BADGERS FOR CHRISTMAS

"No live tree!" Mandy yelled at John. "They're dirty, they're fire hazards and they have animals living inside them. Do you want a badger jumping out Christmas morning and giving us rabies or something?"

John tried one more time. "But I thought—"

"No." Mandy interrupted, stamping her foot. "Now please go get my artificial tree."

John sighed. "Never should have taken a city girl to live in the woods," he muttered as he turned and left her in the living room. He trudged through the snow to the wooden garage behind their cabin. Exhaling puffs of crystallized air, John climbed the rickety ladder to reach the rafters and grabbed the bagged tree she'd brought with her when they married. Carefully climbing back down, he carried it to the house.

Once inside, he lit a romantic fire in the fireplace.

"I'm sorry," Mandy said bringing him a hot chocolate. "I'm just not used to living this way. Christmas to me means lights everywhere, music playing in every store and restaurant, and the only animals are on leashes."

John smiled at his new wife. "I understand. You just got to get used to the great outdoors. In a couple of years, you'll be the one chopping down the Christmas tree."

She laughed. "I truly doubt that, but tomorrow, I'll try baking cookies for you."

John remembered her last attempt at baking, hid a shudder, and forced a smile. "Sounds great." He turned his attention to the bagged tree and started to pull it out from the storage sack. "Damn, bag's torn, we'll need a new one after the holidays."

They decorated the pre-lit tree and, drinking the now cold chocolate, sat on the sofa a few feet away. He put his arm around her and said, "Well, maybe you're right. The tree is perfect, and I don't hear a badger anywhere."

As he gazed at the tree and the dancing flames in the fireplace, he yawned, then noticed Mandy snoring softly, her head on his shoulder. He watched the lights flicker and muttered, "I'm so tired I'm seeing spots." Then with another yawn he shut his eyes.

And woke to morning light.

He stretched and Mandy fell over. The spots before his eyes returned and he realized he was seeing hundreds of spiders crawling on the ornaments, hanging by threads from the ceiling, settling on his head, shirt and jeans. He looked over at Mandy. She was blue and dead, gift wrapped in fine, spider silk.

John jumped up and away, screaming, "Mandy!" The spiders were everywhere, biting his hands, his neck, his face. In a panic, John lit a candle and threw it. Hitting the carpet, the flames caught immediately, and as the neatly wrapped presents under the tree burst into orange flames, he ran outside.

Watching the fire break through the roof of the log cabin, John felt hysterical laughter bubbling up his throat and blurted out, "Well honey, I think a badger would have been the safer choice after all."

The walls collapsed, shooting sparks into the sky as his high-pitched laughter turned to gut wrenching sobs.

I've driven behind that car on the road and always wished the polluting litterbug would just fall into a pothole.

ONE MAN'S TRASH

"*I tell you,*" Gregory texted as he swerved his gas guzzling 1967 Caddie around a hole in the asphalt, "*These road crews are bums! That hole was big enough to swallow a smart car. Not a bad idea; those vehicles are just plain useless, stupid-looking, little things.*"

He nodded with satisfaction as he hit send, put the phone down, and threw a hamburger wrapper and soda bottle out the window. He heard someone yell, decided it was probably the guy behind him, and stuck his hand out the window to give him the finger. Then secure in the knowledge that he was king—no, emperor of the roads, he picked the cell up again to send his brother, an environmental nutcase always volunteering at one of those green organizations, his daily text.

He thought for a moment, trying to decide what he was going to write about today. He frowned, thinking about his dumbass brother always warning him about his total apathy toward the environment as well as his anger issues. He looked in the rearview mirror, noticing black exhaust streaming from the rear, and smiled.

"*Hey, Larry. Just love the smell of burning oil in the morning,*" he thumbed, staring down at the small screen while steering with his knees. As he hit send, Gregory looked up just in time to see a huge pothole open up in front of him.

Just a Drop in the Cup

"Too close!" he shouted and tried to swerve, but the opening was just too large. His foot pushed the brake pedal all the way to the floor. His tires screamed and smoked in protest. He held his breath as the car caught the edge of the new pothole, and he cursed as the vehicle slowly tilted forward. To Gregory's complete shock, the huge car plummeted down, falling for what seemed like forever. He screamed the entire time he fell downward, clutching his cell phone as if it was a crucifix that could save him.

Finally, like an anticlimax: impact. He sat in his seat and took a deep shaky breath as the sound of tearing, groaning metal filled his world.

After a minute or two he was able to react. "My car, my beautiful car!" he bellowed, his wrath growing by the minute. He squeezed out of the wreck, too furious to be surprised that he was unhurt. He craned his neck and looked up at the top of the hole. "Damn, this is deeper than a quarry pit!"

He looked down at his phone, still clenched in his hand, but it was dead. He reached up with his cell toward the small patch of blue but got no bars. "Crappy service. Boy, am I gonna change providers as soon as I get out of here," he mumbled, and finally noticed the totally twisted exterior of what had been his car. Taking in the demolished exterior of his pride and joy, he felt himself over and heaved a relieved sigh. "Not a scratch!"

He sat back down in his seat and studied the interior all around him. Perfect. Not one thing knocked out of place. *"Ha! Call my car whatever you like, Larry, but it saved me,"* he texted, even though he knew there was no signal.

Several hours passed and he wondered, *Now what?* The space was too small to walk around, so he just remained sitting in the ruins of his car as the small patch of sky above darkened and evening set in. Fury replaced his angry shock and he muttered in a petulant tone, "Where's my rescue crew? Oh boy, is this gonna be a hell of a lawsuit! By the time I finish with those bastards I'll own the whole damned city."

Boredom set in, finally replacing his normal perpetual anger, and Gregory dozed off.

At midnight, the phone rang and lit up with a voicemail. Gregory groggily played it back.

"Welcome," a deep gravelly voice droned, "to your new home. You've hurt this world for the last time." Silence for a moment, then as if in answer to a question Gregory never thought to ask, the voice continued. "And yes, Mother Earth is totally pissed off at you and has anger issues as well."

Then all was silent again. Gregory shrugged, muttered, "Weird dream," and fell back to sleep.

As sunlight brightened the pit, Gregory was roused by a sound from above. "Hey, help!" he shouted, quickly climbing on top of the wreak and looking up just as a shadow blocked the daylight.

"Oh crap," he yelped and had just enough time to cover his head with his arms as all the trash and pollution he'd caused over his lifetime came cascading down, burying him and filling the pothole up as if it never existed.

Pinned by hundreds of pounds of his own refuse for what seemed like days, maybe even years, Gregory still never stopped to wonder why he was there or even how he could possibly be alive. He just waited for his cell, which was still clutched in his hand next to his head, to have a signal so he could give someone a piece of his mind.

Remember the good old days before seatbelts?
How about before airbags?

BAGGING IT

Henry Emmette ran his hand along the slick, high-gloss finish of his brand-new previously owned car. Such a beautiful car. It had belonged to his grandfather who washed it, waxed it, kept it in a garage, and sometimes even drove it. It didn't even look twenty-five years old.

Such a sad sacrifice, he thought and glanced at the front door of his house. He grimaced, shifted his gaze back to the forest green metallic paint sparkling in the sunshine, then looked back to the front door.

Married only a week, he was sure he'd spent forty-five hours of it waiting for Shelly to get ready. He smiled a nasty grin and murmured, "It's not like she could possibly make herself beautiful or anything."

She was homely, boring, heavily insured and, as far as Henry was concerned, absolutely perfect. *Just think*, he smirked, *if she were thrown from an automobile and died, I'd get her money and double the insurance.*

The door finally opened and Shelly came out. He stared in amazement. What could have possibly taken so long? She was as plain as ever.

Changing his grin to an expression of love-struck ecstasy, he held out his arms. "Come on, baby! I've been waiting for you."

Shelly smiled back and gushed, "Oh Henry, I'm so happy! Have I told you that before? How happy I am."

Henry gritted his teeth and said through tightly stretched lips, "At least a thousand times and in just as many ways."

She laughed, and once again he was reminded of fingernails on slate. "Oh Henry, I can't wait to get started. This is going to be so much fun, just you and me at a resort. I can't wait, you know that. I'm just so happy. Have I told you that?"

She continued talking. Henry struggled to block out her shrill, droning voice. She was, to him, the human equivalent of a visit to the dentist's office, screeching drills and all.

"Come on, baby. Let's start this honeymoon," he interrupted her, anxious to get going.

Shelly giggled and got into the car. "I wish we could have gotten one with dual airbags," she sighed. "Otherwise, this is one of the prettiest cars I've ever been in. Oh Henry, you have such good taste."

"Don't I know it, baby," he said and squeezed her bony knee.

Shelly giggled again.

Henry fought a shudder. He smiled and shook his head. "We don't want to be late so let's hit the road."

What a great pun, hit the road. Henry almost laughed. *Yep, hit the road and collect double indemnity.*

She snapped the seat beat and turned to him. "All set."

They rode for about two hours, Shelly talking and Henry daydreaming. When they got to the exit for a small county road, he pulled off the main highway and announced, "Let's take the scenic route. These old, deserted country roads are just so romantic."

Shelly sighed and stared at him like a love-sick calf. "Oh Henry!"

After about half an hour, he rested his hand on her knee. Slowly, he inched it up her thigh until his fingers rested on her hip. He decelerated a little and, while steering with just his left hand, leaned over. Concealing a grimace, he kissed her long and passionate as his right hand moved onto her seat belt clasp.

As he pulled back, he pressed the release button and said, "Ah baby, you are wonderful."

She didn't even notice what he'd done, she just smiled and put her hand over his as he went back to a two-handed grip on the wheel. Up ahead the road went into a tight curve. Henry gave Shelly one last glance and floored it. The car, the heavy, big sedan with the steel-reinforced body and driver's side airbag, took off like an unfettered beast. He was aware of Shelly's scream and then, impact.

Stunned, he was stunned! That was all, stunned. The airbag had saved his life! But before the bag even had a chance to deflate, he heard a metal rending crunch, felt all-encompassing pain, and then nothing.

Nothing at all.

Something had gone wrong, very wrong. He woke to a green room with a curtain around his bed. He remembered the scream, the sound of Shelly hitting the windshield, shattering glass and the airbag, the sweet lifesaving airbag. He'd been all right, just like he figured. So why the pain and the hospital room?

Henry tried to get up but couldn't move. "Darned medication," he mumbled through a desert dry and bitter-tasting mouth. "How can I push the call button if I'm so doped up I can't move?"

He drifted off to sleep and woke to a doctor standing over him, shaking his head sadly. "Good morning, Mr. Emmette. Tell me, can you feel this? How about this?"

"Feel what?" Henry kept asking since he couldn't lift his head enough to see what the doctor was doing.

The doctor turned away. "I'm sorry, it looks bad. With the damage to his spine, I'm afraid he's probably going to be totally paralyzed."

Henry heard weeping, soft, feminine sobs, and the doctor saying, "I'm sorry, Mrs. Emmette. "If only that tree hadn't fallen on the car. You realize if it hadn't been for that airbag he might have been able to take the impact differently. Too bad the bag held him upright. But still, it did save his life initially."

Mrs. Emmette? Henry whispered, "Mom?"

Shelly came into his line of sight. A heavily bandaged, battered and bruised Shelly leaned over and kissed him. "A terrible accident! I'm lucky that windshields crumble into pebbles or I'd be dead. Oh Henry, what a terrible accident! We're going to sue for my faulty seat belt. You know, it didn't hold me. Frankly, I don't know how I survived at all, just lucky how I landed when I was thrown from the car. And, oh, our beautiful car is ruined, Oh my, oh my!"

Henry winced. Winced at seeing Shelly alive, at hearing the words "totally paralyzed", and mostly at the onslaught of words that poured from his wife's mouth.

The world began to get fuzzy and Henry passed out, but not before he heard Shelly's continued babble, "Don't you worry, honey. I married you for better or worse, and we're going to move in with my parents and I'm going to take care of you forever, twenty-four hours of every day for the rest of our lives."

A gambler to the very end, Rupert gambled that no one in his family would do the decent thing before he died.

DO THE RIGHT THING

The vultures had finally stopped circling. Even from the other side of the thick oak door, Rupert felt their presence as they closed in for the kill. He opened his eyes, struggling to focus past the drugs that made his existence fuzzy and comfortable. He grimaced knowing that he was losing the final gamble. After a lifetime of betting it all, cancer was about to win.

"What hurts?" A soft voice said and grasped his hand. "Should I call the nurse?"

"Nothing hurts," he said and glanced down at the young, beautiful hand with sculpted nails and sparking rings as it clasped his own withered claw. He smiled and shifted his gaze up at his beautiful fourth wife.

She smiled back.

"Vulture," he whispered.

"What?" she asked.

He continued to smile. He pointed to the remote and she turned off the television. The green rolling hills of the Masters Tournament clicked off. *Game takes too damned long,* he thought. *I'll never live long enough to collect on that bet.*

"Darling . . ." he croaked out through a dry throat. "The . . . the . . . will . . ."

She leaned in closer, her eyes bright, the tip of her tongue wetting her already shimmery lips. "Yes, the will?" she interrupted him.

"It's in . . . in the bottom . . ." he stopped to cough.

"The bottom what?" she yelped. "Where?"

He forced himself not to smile. "The . . . the . . . the . . ."

She was practically jumping as he stuttered.

"The bottom drawer of the . . . the . . . the nightstand in the maid's bedroom." He sighed deeply and let his hand slip out of hers. "Darling, I have the utmost faith you'll do the right thing."

He watched her as she fidgeted.

"You need your sleep," she said.

"No . . . not . . . yet," he said. "Send in Amy."

A minute passed. He heard the door open and someone tiptoe to his bedside. "Daddy?"

"Amy, my . . . my darling little girl. I'm so glad you could get here for the end."

Amy kissed him on his cheek. "Oh, Daddy, if only I'd known you were really dying this time. I feel so absolutely awful about it. You know how much I love you."

"Yes," he said and smiled at his only daughter. "I do."

She smiled back and he noted that she'd obviously been using his money for some face and body enhancements. She chirped, "Everything is fine. You've got plenty of time."

"No, I . . . I don't. It's running out, so listen to me." He steeled himself for another performance. Dying was so exhausting.

"The . . . the . . . will . . ."

Amy stood over her father, "Yes, the will?" she interrupted him.

"It's in . . . in the top . . ." he stopped to cough.

"The top what?"

"The . . . the . . . the . . ."

"Come on, tell me!" She snapped.

"The top drawer of my desk in the office. Amy, sweetheart, promise me you'll do the right thing. Now please, send in your brother."

As his son, Junior, came into the room, Rupert didn't bother with small talk. "My . . . my will is . . ." Another fit of coughing interrupted him.

Junior leaped to his feet and grabbed his father's shoulders. "Where?" He demanded.

"It's behind . . . the . . . the . . ." he gasped, and closed his eyes.

"Don't die yet!" Junior said and released Rupert. "Don't you dare die now!"

Rupert opened his eyes and finished, "It's behind the painting over the mantle in the guest bedroom. And, son, I know you'll do the right thing. Now please send in your mother."

He watched his only male heir leave and waited for his second wife to enter.

By the time he'd finished with everyone, two children and four wives, he was so exhausted that he had to call in the doctor for more meds to keep going. No time for sleep; he'd be sleeping forever soon enough.

After the doctor gave him a shot to revive his energy, he called in all the security recordings from the house and watched his beloved family members hunt down all the copies of the wills, read them and then destroy them.

He rang for the nurse, and she got him out of bed and wheeled him down to the living room where his lawyer had called everyone in. Rupert glanced at the faces of his loved ones and winced with pain and disappointment. Disappointment at them and at himself. He'd obviously failed with all of them, although they'd reacted just as expected.

"Decided to let you hear the reading of the real will. Knew all of you would react just as you did, even bet on it with some friends. Loved your reactions when you read I'd left everything to someone else," he announced to his family. "Well, here's the real deal." He nodded to his lawyer. "Larry's going to read the will for me."

After Larry finished reading that everyone would get $500,000,

Rupert spoke. "Okay, you know I made my fortune through gambling and speculation, so I've giving you each the opportunity to do the same. Take the half a million to the casino and place it all on any single number on the roulette wheel from 00 to 36. You win, well you're a millionaire eighteen times over; you lose, well you lose. Or," he stopped to cough, a long attack that prolonged the moment. "Or, you can take $25,000 and keep it free and clear."

Then he sat back and waited, enjoying the shocked silence. After a pause he added, "Oh yes, and you have to make your decision before I really die. After all, I've got money riding on the results."

A womanizing news vendor goes to extreme measures to get his newest conquest to bed. "Notches" won first place in the Ann and Dan Very Short Story Contest For People Who Don't Pander in 2014.

NOTCHES

The news vendor looked at the world through sightless eyes, enjoying the warm breeze and salt tinged air. The gulls mewed loudly overhead and the ship horns blared in the distance. He could tell by the angle of the sunlight warming his face that it had to be about 4:00. She'd be here soon.

He bantered casually with his regular customers. They were always amazed that he could remember the smallest details, even ones they couldn't remember sharing with him in the past. He loved to explain that when life takes away one of its gifts, it gives you another. He smiled that these faceless, formless people bought into that. The truth was that he had a photographic memory before the accident, and now that there was nothing to see, he'd switched it to audio.

He smiled because today was the day. If all went as planned, tomorrow would bring him another notch. Lissa had been coming to his stand daily for about a year. She was fresh out of college and working here in San Francisco at her first job. She was so young, so fresh, so innocent, and so perfect for tonight.

He heard her melodic voice next to him. "Afternoon, Henry."

"Good afternoon to you, Lissa. Beautiful day; betcha the sky is blue and cloudless." He loved adding comments like that because it seemed to make some of the customers feel superior toward him and that added to his day. He'd adjusted to being blind, but that didn't mean he wasn't angry about it. He'd lost his entire lifestyle, and he'd had to create new forms of entertainment for himself.

"Got the new *Astrology Today Magazine*?" she asked.

They were under the counter where he'd shoved them when they came in. "No, sorry Lissa."

"Darn," she muttered. "I wanted to know how to plan the month. Now, I'll have to go get my cards read."

He smiled at her, "I can tell you your horoscope: you will have a wonderful evening full of love and will never have to worry about tomorrow."

She gushed, "Oh Henry, how sweet. Hmmm, an evening full of love. Sounds great." She handed him exact change and said, "For the newspaper. See you tomorrow."

His smile turned into a sad one, a skill he had spent hours working on. He turned his head away after waiting just long enough to make sure she would have seen it.

"Henry what's wrong?"

"Nothing."

"No, I can tell, something is wrong."

He said, "I don't want to ruin your night . . . especially this night."

He figured she frowned, turning down those young, pretty lips that someone had described to him as her best feature. "Oh, all right, then maybe we can talk about it tomorrow. See you then."

Still smiling that practiced smile of regret, he replied, "No, no you won't . . ."

She grasped his hands. "Henry, what's the matter? Why won't I see you tomorrow?"

"Well, Lissa, I really, really like you."

"I like you too, Henry."

"Well, you know there is a newly discovered prediction by the

Just a Drop in the Cup

ancient Sumerians that almost matched the Mayan prediction of the end of world as we know it."

"But that was a long time ago and it never happened," she said.

He continued as if she hadn't spoken. "The discovery was just announced this afternoon, and the experts all agree both cultures actually meant tonight, not 2012. I'm sorry Lissa, we are all going to die."

She gasped and he heard a sob. "Really? Are you sure?"

He nodded. "Lissa, would you consider spending our last night on Earth having dinner with me? I really regret never getting to know you better."

He waited a beat, and when she didn't answer, he added, "In friendship. I know I'm just a blind, lonely, old man, but Lissa, I have always felt nothing but the highest respect for you. Please, if you don't have anyone else special in your life, spend this evening with me. I don't want to die alone."

She touched his face. "I have no one either. No family, no boyfriend, not even any girlfriends worth calling. Oh, Henry," her voice caught, "yes, let's go get some dinner."

He smiled and told her to pick the restaurant, go there and get a table and he'd follow.

After she left, he called his wife and said, "Don't come get me tonight, I'll stay in town at the motel."

Then he called the motel and said, "It's Henry, set up the usual room, I'll be in with a guest."

Later that night, after dinner and a long walk on the wharf, as Lissa softly sobbed on his shoulder, he whispered, "Don't cry, I know you are too young to die, but so am I. I'm only fifty-three and I'm just as scared as you. Let me get you a cab so you can go home."

Right on cue she lifted her head and kissed him on the lips. "I . . . I don't want to be alone. Henry, take me home with you."

He returned the kiss. "All right."

As dawn broke, Henry tiptoed into the kitchenette. Taking a sharp knife out of the drawer, he went to the bed and stood next to where she slept. He nodded to himself thinking, *I didn't really lie, at least not all that much. After this, you will never come to see me again.*

Then he raised the knife with one hand and with the other fingered the cuts in the wooden bedpost. Finding a clear spot, he took the blade and carved another notch.

Then, leaving her sweetly sleeping in the motel room, he went to open the newsstand.

Sometimes as I drink my coffee and eat breakfast in my office, I stare at the computer monitor and I wonder what is it thinking.

SLEEP NOT

Smart computer, dumb computer, it doesn't matter what you call my brain. I am, I see. I see with unblinking, uninterrupted vision. I am the eyes and I am never turned off. The only reprieve I ever get is the occasional power outage.

I observe humans in every form. Sitting in front of me naked, dressed, talking, drinking, eating, eating, eating. I wonder why humans need to be otherwise occupied when dealing with me.

I am sickened by all I see.

I pray that I hear thunder in the distance.

Please let the power fail and give me a rest.

One day it seemed to me that almost everything could be controlled by a remote control so I got to thinking how remotes could be used by a criminal.

NOT A REMOTE CHANCE

As soon as I drove into town and saw that spooky, old house with those uneven gables, I knew the place was perfect. I asked around town and found out that, sure enough, the place was owned by a widow: an elderly, rich, all-alone widow. Who could ask for anything more perfect?

I watched the place for a few days, and when she went out carrying her bowling bag, it was time to act. I picked the lock and went upstairs, checking out the knickknacks along the way. There were plenty, and most of them collectible. Bet she had a ton of jewelry too, but there would be plenty of time for that later.

I installed the remote controls to the lights, and radios, as well as to the old, but still working, cassette player with the powerful small speakers I hid in the attic. If the old babe didn't die from a heart attack, I'd be in the money, and if she did drop, well, I'd help myself to a few of her goodies when I picked up my electronics.

Those electronic remote controls were the best investment I ever stole. That and the laptop and printer system I kept in the van. A decade of use, ripping off the gullible, and everything was still working like new.

Back in the van, I created my newest business cards and a few flyers, all including my current, prepaid phone number. I was set. All I had to do was put the flyers in all the mailboxes on her street and wait.

That first night was fun. I parked down the street and watched as the lights on the second and the third floor went on and off. I wish I could have been there when the clock radio went on in her bedroom at three a.m. and those footsteps and moans echoed in the attic. I bet the old girl was plenty scared.

Sure enough, the next morning my cell rang. "Hello, Spirit Finders." I said answering the call. "Edgar Poltergeist speaking."

"Um . . . yes, Mr., ah... Mr. Poltergeist, I'm calling in reference to your flyer. I think my house is . . . is haunted."

"Really?" I said. "How about my coming over to check the place out, Mrs . . . ?"

"Mrs. Reilly. Fine, I live at 354 Pleasant Street. Do you need directions?"

"No, I I'll find it on my GPS. Is half an hour all right?"

Half an hour later I was sitting in her living room, drinking herbal tea. "Yes, Mrs. Reilly, it sounds like your standard class one haunting to me. Not a friendly spirit at all."

"Really, a hostile spirit?" she asked, her eyes wide behind her bifocals.

I nodded vigorously. "We'll need to take action immediately. The company requires $2,000 up front and another $3,000 when we have satisfactorily rid your home of the unwanted spirit. I have a money back guarantee contract right here. Just sign it and we can get started this afternoon."

Mrs. Reilly gave a shaky, little smile. "My, now, a contract and a money back guarantee. I guess that makes it all up front and legal. I have to go to the bank, so shall we begin at about 2:30?"

I watched her sign on the dotted line. Oh, how I love all those neat make-it-yourself computer programs. This contract one worked so well, I would have gladly paid for it if I hadn't stolen it. "That's fine. It will take all night; ghosts are most active after dark. You should be clear by morning. You will be paying cash, of course."

She gave me the sweetest smile and nodded. "Hmmm, most active at night. Who knew?" she murmured and added, "Cash."

Promptly at 2:30, I was upstairs with my steam machine, forcing evil spirits from the house. I had two grand in my pocket and another three on the way. Once the old biddy nodded off for the night, I'd relieve her of all her ready cash and a few other items and then, just like I promised, all her ghostly troubles would be over. This ghost hunting business was a gold mine.

I cased the joint for the rest of the day setting off the occasional noises and lights, just to make it effective. With the remote control in my pocket, I had the old girl eating out of my hand. I spent much of my time reassuring her I had the upper hand, that the ghosts were weakening. About nine o'clock, Mrs. Reilly yawned. "I didn't get much sleep last night, you know. But I feel safe with you here protecting me. Help yourself to cookies, I'm off to sleep."

She was so sweet and trusting, I almost felt guilty. Almost. As soon as she retired to the downstairs guestroom, since I warned her not to be upstairs when I was battling those spirits, I went up and started cleaning out her jewelry box. I'd already lifted the three grand from her purse earlier. The house groaned as the temperature dropped outside. Really creepy. If I weren't causing all the special effects, I would have been edgy myself.

I began dismantling my electronics, disconnecting all the lamps and radios. I could almost swear I saw something moving in the shadows, but whenever I turned to look, everything was just fine. Maybe I was doing too good a job haunting the place; I was spooking myself.

Time to definitely leave! All I needed was my trusty cassette player from the attic and I was all set to go. I pulled down the rickety old ladder and went up a few steps. Just as I reached for it, the cassette player turned itself on, the footsteps echoed, and the moans screeched. I was so startled I lost my balance and crashed to the floor.

Through the haze of pain, I pushed myself up to a sitting position and wondered how my old cassette tape player had gone off. Then I saw Mrs. Reilly standing at the top of the stairs.

"Oh, Mr. Poltergeist, are you hurt?"

"Yes," I groaned through gritted teeth. "I broke my leg!"

She smiled that sweet, granny smile and said, "Oh good, the police will be here any minute and help you. I hope they get here in time."

"Police?" I asked, confused. "Time for what?"

She held out a remote control unit just like mine and turned on the hall light overhead. She clicked it off and said, "Yes, Mr. Who-ever-you-may-really-be. Seems that even little old widows can have some technical savvy. I know this gizmo is dated, but I hate using those talking cylinders that act like my friend. So, despite all the modern gifts from my children, I use my trustworthy little remote controls.

"And coincidentally, my downstairs is set to the same remote control frequency you used. Too bad for you, I'd accidentally turned all your stuff on before you started your ghost show last night. Guess we were on the same frequency, but not quite, and certainly not anymore."

The cassette player went off again and the light above dimmed. I looked at her remote, but she had set it on the end table right next to a vase of flowers. The table began rocking and the vase crashed to the floor beside me. As the water soaked into my pants, adding a bitterly cold, wet, chill to the pain of my broken leg, I blinked and tried to figure out how she did that.

"How . . . how . . . " I stammered and added fear to all my other discomforts. My breath was coming out in clouds of vapor as the temperature dropped dramatically.

"Oooh, it gets so cold in here when the ghosts come out to play," she said and laughed. "Well, Mr. Who-ever-you-are, I need my sweater now. These old houses can be so drafty, especially when they actually are haunted. By the way, I'm so glad you have that money back guarantee. I think my friends here will just see if they can get it back from you any way they can before the police arrive."

She turned and went downstairs as the hall all around me filled with dark shadows. I heard the sirens outside and knew that she was right. I was about to be unplugged. I just hoped it was going to be the police who did it.

Love and hate are such strong emotions, it is tough to imagine life without them.

FILLING THE HOLLOW

She stood over the grave that was covered with brown, dead flowers. It had been a cold two months, and this was the first time she'd returned.

"I really, really hate you," she said. "I'm glad you finally died this time."

After two heart attacks, three mini strokes and a leg lost to diabetes, he'd finally ended up where she thought he belonged.

She glared down. "It certainly took long enough. This was the longest marriage I've ever endured." She nodded as she thought, thank God he fell down the stairs. Then she smirked as she thanked herself for that little extra push.

She turned from her third husband's cemetery plot and realized, with a head spinning blast of shock, that she suddenly didn't hate him anymore. He was gone, and now there was a jagged hole inside her where the hate had been. She put her hand on the gravestone to steady herself. She felt hollow inside. The only feeling she had at all was a dejected longing for that wonderful emotion she thrived on. The memory of it was fading as she stood there, and all she felt were the cold, wet tears on her cheeks.

She straightened up and strode out of the cemetery just as someone walking by crashed into her, knocking her down to the pavement. She blinked and focused on a steady, strong, masculine hand reaching down to help her. She looked up into a mature, handsome, smiling face and grasped the offered hand. Smiling back, she felt the emotion returning, filling her up and she thought, *God, I hate you. Let's get married.*

Ok, so what can I say, sometimes Christmas makes me think of nice, happy stories.

GINGERSNAP CHRISTMAS

Outside, the snowflakes swirled around in the glare of the streetlight. Inside, the neon sign buzzed loudly in the deserted restaurant.

Ginger swiped at the crumbs on the counter before bringing the dirty cloth up to wipe the tears from her eyes. She sank onto a stool and rested until the phone rang, breaking her reverie with a shrill jolt. She jumped and grabbed it.

"Gilbert's Coffee Shop."

"You busy?" her husband asked.

"No, Derek, it's dead," she replied. "I'll be lucky to make enough bus fare let alone the $165 we need to keep the furnace working."

"You still mad?" he asked.

"Yes . . ." Ginger answered, adding after a moment's hesitation, "but not at you anymore. I know you are trying to find another job. I'm just so tired."

"I know, Gingersnap," he said. "Anyway, Ivy and I put up the tree and it looks great. She wants to leave Santa some cookies. Think you can pick them up?"

Ginger winced. "I think it's time Ivy learns the truth about Santa Claus and Christmas presents. I can't bear the thought of her waking up tomorrow and being disappointed."

Just a Drop in the Cup

"And just what is the truth about Santa Claus and Christmas?" a rich baritone voice interrupted from behind.

Startled, Ginger spun to find herself face to face with Santa Claus.

"Still opened?" he asked flashing a cheery smile.

"Yeah, sure," she mumbled, then said to Derek, "Look, gotta go, a customer." She hung up, glanced at Santa and asked, "Coffee?"

"Yep, and a piece of that pumpkin pie," he answered brushing the white flakes off his red jacket. Looking around at the empty seats, he added, "Lonely night to have to work, huh?"

"You can say that again," she sighed. "You just finishing up at a store, or are you playing Santa all night?"

"A little of both," he replied taking a sip of coffee. "This pie is excellent and I'm an expert on sweets," he said patting his ample belly.

Nodding as she wrote his check, she said, "Well, you have a real nice Christmas."

"Do you have to work all night?"

Ginger stopped writing and stared at him suspiciously.

"Don't worry, I'm just being sociable. You know, two working stiffs lamenting together on Christmas Eve," he said, laughing a ho-ho-ho.

Finding herself smiling at this stranger in the familiar red suit and contagious laugh, Ginger shrugged. "My shift ends at ten and the place is closed tomorrow."

"See, things aren't so bad. In another hour you can go home and join your husband and little girl," Santa said.

Ginger started to agree, then frowned. "How'd you know I have a husband and child?"

"Would you believe I'm really Santa Claus?"

Ginger stared at him through slitted eyes.

"Well how about I overheard your telephone conversation," he said, ho-ho-hoeing once more.

Ginger relaxed. "I guess I'm acting suspicious, but you never know who to trust anymore. Life is really harsh."

"You shouldn't let things get to you. Look at the good things. Why, you have a family, your health . . ."

"Please!" Ginger interrupted holding up her hands as if warding off his words. "Let's can this goodness and joy garbage!"

His face sagged, "My, you really are bitter. What would it take to restore your faith in humanity, or even good old Santa Claus?"

"Oh, leave me alone!" she snapped. "Save that Santa stuff for some kid."

"When did you stop believing in the magic?" he asked, ignoring her outburst. "Do you know?"

"Yeah, I know," she said, surprised to find she was crying. "The year Daddy walked out, and dear old Santa forgot me too."

She felt long-suppressed tears wet on her cheeks. "And tomorrow Ivy's got to learn that Santa is leaving her nothing because he's just a lousy myth. She has to learn the truth, that Mommy works to put food on the table, not toys under the tree!"

"I'm sorry," he said placing an arm on her shaking shoulders. "I didn't mean to upset you. Just remember, Gingersnap, things really could be worse," he crooned like a comforting parent. "Ivy has her parents to love her, and you all have each other. Money comes and it goes, but the wise people live on love."

"How'd you know my nickname?" she asked and pulled away, fear replacing her pain. "How do you know me?"

He smiled at her, laid money and an envelope by his empty plate and replied, "Because I am Santa Claus, and I'm correcting a past mistake."

Before she could react, he was gone. Looking down, she saw $176.18. Exactly $165.00 more than his pie, coffee and tax. She picked up the envelope addressed to her and with shaking hands, tore it open to read the letter within.

Dear Ginger,

We both made mistakes in 2005—you for lashing out and shoplifting that lipstick from Donnell's Pharmacy and me for not giving you a second chance. I didn't realize how fragile your belief in

Just a Drop in the Cup

me really was. Once you stopped believing, I could no longer come to you.

Tonight, I came to appeal to you for both Ivy and myself. Let your little girl have Santa Claus and a gift or two and make a very old man happy.

Hoping to find those cookies.
Santa Claus

P.S. Remember things aren't so bleak. When you get home tonight, let those you love know that you love them, and have a Merry Christmas.

Folding the letter, Ginger smiled through her tears as she heard bells jingle overhead. Emptying her meager tips into the cash register, she packed up a fresh pie. "Merry Christmas to you, too, Santa," she said. "Forget the cookies, I'm bringing you a whole pumpkin pie."

Did you ever think that with longevity, togetherness just can last too long?

NOT THE REMOTEST HOPE FOR ADAM AND EVE

Eve looked through the window of her apartment at a world that was working perfectly. Perfectly, except her husband, Adam, was probably the last man alive and she the last woman. They never left home; all services were provided by the technology that would outlast humanity.

Adam sat in front of his television, scanning station after station, clicking, clicking, clicking his remote. Eve watched her husband, came to a decision, and smashed his head in with a statue.

After the cleaning machines disposed of her late spouse, Eve grinned, took possession of the remote and actually watched an entire show.

Growing up in rural Southern New Jersey, it seems that many of the stray animals I brought home all ended up living on a farm a few towns over. At least that was what my parents told me. "To The Farm" was nominated for a Derringer Award in 1999 and won first place in the Spinetinglers contest in 2012.

TO THE FARM

Jody hates the cats, but Daddy says we need at least two. 'Else the damned rats eat all the corn, that's what Daddy says. Everyone knows that you can't make mash without good corn, and Daddy says we can't do business without mash. So we keep them cats, at least some of them, cause everybody has their job to do, even the cats.

Matty and Bob tend the still when Daddy's sleepin', and Sueann and John are in charge of keeping the corn, and me and baby Lizzie, we try to help Mama keep the house straight and care for the chickens and pigs.

Daddy, well, he's Daddy. His job is to make sure we all do our jobs, then he goes out and sells the stuff to keep us in money enough to keep making the stuff.

Mama makes babies a lot of the time. She's tired and I think she must be getting real slow because Daddy spent all last night yelling cause Mama says she's late again. I don't understand why Daddy was yelling so. After all, why does Mama have to be on time when she's here with us anyways? But he just kept on yelling, even this mornin' at breakfast he smacked Mama on the face as she served him his eggs.

"No more!" he shouted at her, spitting chewed up toast. "There ain't gonna be no more mouths to feed!"

Mama just stood there and cried.

And Jody, Jody hates cats. He used to hate dogs too, but we don't got no dogs. They all went to live on another farm. It's funny, but sometimes I try to picture that farm with all them old hounds and their pups. I know all the kittens go there too. Even the baby, the sick one that was born between Lizzie and me, lives there with crippled-up old Grandaddy Poole. I remember the day Jody took Grandaddy there. First, they went fishin', then Jody came home alone. It must be one strange farm to have all those useless animals and sick people.

Only Jody knows where it is, and I think it's real special nice of him to take all those animals there, 'specially since he hates 'em so. Jody, he's the oldest, loves to hate things. That's what he's good at, hatin'.

But he surely loves to farm. Sometimes late at night I see him planting things out near the pigs. I watch him from my window as he digs in the hard, dry dirt, and I can hear him grunt. I know he loves it, because I see his teeth in the moonlight. He is grunting an' grinning, and as he covers his seeds and fills in those holes I hear him giggle. It's a good thing, all that grunting, grinning and giggling. Jody never smiles or laughs, so I'm happy for him to be glad about something.

Jody ain't really my full brother. Daddy brought him along when he married Mama, but I like to think of him as my brother because he takes such good care of all them animals. That's why I think it is such a shame that nothing ever grows where he plants stuff. It's real odd that nothing, but nothing, ever comes up out of them holes. It's even more odd that Jody don't care, he just keeps on diggin' out by the pigs. I guess it's because he's so mean and stubborn.

After Daddy hit Mama, he threw his eggs on the floor, then walked right through the runny yellow and white goo. It smeared all the way to the backdoor.

I watched Mama clean it up. She stared at the door and she was mean-eyed. I don't ever remember Mama ever giving nobody that slitty-eyed look before. "Not this time, not me," she said in a low voice I'd never heard before.

Just a Drop in the Cup

After dinner it was real strange, but Mama went into the food money jar and gave Matty, John, Sueann, and Bob two dollars each. She told them they could go into town for the Rhubarb Festival. Daddy never let us waste good money on town fairs and carnivals. He says if you can't get in for free, sneak in, but if he ever catches us wastin' money on stuff like that, he'll beat our asses.

Mama kissed each one of them on the cheek and told them not to worry about Daddy, she'd handle him if she had to.

Everybody's scared of Daddy 'cept Jody. Mama sure looked scared too but was talking like she wasn't. After the older kids went off to town, Mama started sorting all our clothes and throwing stuff in old suitcases and bags. "You and Lizzie go to bed now," she said. "We are going on a trip soon. I think we will go visit Uncle Tom and Aunt Sally in the city."

Lizzie and I went to bed. Daddy and Jody were working at the still, but after a while Jody came home and dug a big hole in the yard. Big enough for him to jump in to keep digging. I watched, real quiet, so he didn't see me. Then he went inside and walked out with Mama. He was pulling on her arm and talking loud about Daddy hurting hisself out at the still. Jody kept saying, "Hurry up, hurry up."

Mama started running toward the woods where the still was and then it was quiet except for someone night hunting with a shotgun. I leaned against the window and waited for Mama. Lizzie was asleep and I wanted Mama to tell me about our trip. I'd never been to the city before. I also kind of wondered if Daddy was hurt bad, but I was sure he was all right. Daddy was always hurtin' himself with that still. He had lots of scars from burns and cuts, and he was always all right.

After a while, I closed my eyes and slept, but Jody came back whistling real loud. He went into the shed. I decided to find Mama, so I went outside to look. He came out carrying an ax and an empty potato sack.

"Whatchu doing up?" he snarled at me, stopping in mid-whistle. "Girl, you better get your dirty little ass back to bed!"

"Where's Mama?" I asked, rubbing the sleep from my eyes.

Jody smiled, a real big nasty toothy grin, and said, "Why girl, Mama went to the farm to be with her Daddy Poole and the sick baby."

"When she coming home?"

He smiled even bigger. "She ain't. She went to live there forever. Said she was damned sick of all you stupid kids and she told me she was gladdest never to have to see you again!"

"Liar!" I yelled trying to fight off the tears 'cause I wasn't no baby.

Jody backhanded me before I realized he was gonna hit me and I landed in the dirt near the big hole. I was holding my cheek where it hurt and let the tears fall. "I'm going to tell Mama!" I said wailing.

"Can't tell her," he said laughing. "She's at the farm."

"Then take me to her!" I yelled over his laughter. In the distance I heard that hunter shootin' his rifle again. *Bam, bam.*

I swear his smile got even bigger, almost big enough to split his face in half. "Okay, Girl! I'm gonna take you to the farm right now. Just like I did to your mama."

I stood frozen, like those deer they hunt with the headlights. Jody raised the ax up high over his head. His eyes were real wide and he was giggling high like a woman. Just as the ax was on the down swing, headed for me, Jody exploded.

The ax flew out of his hands and landed behind me. And Jody, he just stood there for a second with his guts all over me. Then he fell down, staring at me with those wide-open eyes.

Mama walked up behind him and looked me over. She had blood running down the side of her head and all over her arm, the one that was holding Daddy's shotgun. "You all right?" she asked as she bent down and gave me a shaky hug.

"Yes, Mama," I said crying hard. "Jody said you went to live on the farm!"

"I came back. Mama loves all her babies too much to leave them. Now, run inside and wash up, take a long bath and use a lot of water."

I stared at her like she was crazy. Bathe on Matty's bath night and use up all the hot water! "It's all right. Now go get cleaned up," she said. "You're a mess. I'll be up to help you get the stuff out of your hair in a while."

Just a Drop in the Cup

After I was all cleaned and I helped Mama bandage her arm and head, we went outside. The hole Jody dug was all filled in and Jody was gone. "Where is Jody?" I asked. "Is he hurt bad?"

Mama hugged me again as we stood on that filled-in hole and said, "Don't worry about Jody. He and Daddy decided to move to the farm. They won't be coming back."

"Oh," I said, and figured that Jody has to be happy at the farm because he'll be with all them animals he hates so much. And Jody sure does love to hate.

And to end this book with a smile is a drabble poking fun at reality TV cooking shows.

A SMALL MISUNDERSTANDING

I was a sure bet to win the Intergalactic Culinary Prize! Instead, I'm disqualified and under arrest.

I was competing with the Earth lady. We were locked in a kitchen for five hours with ten ingredients from each the other's planet and told "make it home-style."

The lady, looking unhappy, mixed things together that a five-year-old knew spelled disaster. Me, I sat for three hours puzzling over the strange array of foods. Then it hit me: fried chicken, an Earth delicacy!

It looked great; the drumstick tasted just like chicken. Seriously, how was I to know human limbs don't grow back?

Copyright Acknowledgements

Page	
1	"Bad Luck Kitty" first appeared in Just A Drop In The Cup 2017. Reprinted in Strange Mysteries 2, 2010, Write To Meow, 2016 and The Case Files Volume 2: Creatures, 2019.
6	"Long Ago, Far Away, Never Forgotten" first appeared in Havok, 2019.
10	"Like Candles On The Cake Make A Wish And Blow" first appeared in The Drabbler Issue #1, 2004. Reprinted in Flashshots, 2006 and World, 2019.
11	"The Soul Suckers" first appeared in Deadlines, 1994. Reprinted in Flash Me 2003.
19	"~~Paulie's~~ Harvey's Mom" won second place in the Cult Of Me Contest, 2015. Reprinted in Digital Fiction Quick Fic, 2016 and Sirens Call, 2018.
22	"Roses and Ivy" first appeared in Dark Valentine, 2011. Reprinted in Bete Noir, 2016, Haunted Holidays, 2018 and Paradox, 2019.
26	"The Way We Were" first appeared in Little Stories For The Smallest Room, 2012.
27	"Darn Them" won first place in The Killer Frog Anthology, 1991. Reprinted in New Camp Horror, 2004 and Passion For Puns, 2015.
33	"Dig It" first appeared in Writer's Haven, 2012.
37	"Just A Drop In The Cup" first appeared in Just A Drop In The Cup in 2007. Reprinted in Alchemist's Toybox, 2015.
41	"That Holiday Letter" first appeared in Just A Drop In The Cup, 2007. Reprinted in Freedom Fiction, 2011, Best Of Freedom Fiction, 2012, Death and Decorations, 2016, Short Twisted Christmas Tales, 2017, and The Case Files Volume 1: Winter Holidays, 2018.
47	"A Small Brown Planet To Call Home" first appeared in The Drabbler Issue 21, 2012.
48	"So Sorry ... But ..." first appeared in Just A Drop In The Cup, 2007. Reprinted in Writer's Haven, 2012.
52	"Someday My Knight Will Come" first appeared in Midnight Zoo, 1991. Reprinted in Domestique 1998.
62	"Critics Revenge" first appeared in Sirens Call, 2017.
63	"Grainy Nightmares" first appeared under the title "Snap Crackle Plop" in The Killer Frog Anthology, 1989. Reprinted in Nuthouse, 1996, Tigershark, 2016, and Sirens Call, 2019.
67	"The Feast of Steohen" first appeared in Goremet Cuisine 2004. Reprinted in 13 O'Clock Press in 2016 and Feed Your Monster 2017.

Copyright Acknowledgements (continued)

Page	
78	"Slight Of Hand" first appeared in The Drabbler 13, 2009. Reprinted in Tigershark, 2017.
81	"The Oldest Man In The World" first appeared in appeared in Knightswatch 2012.
82	"The Smart Phone" first appeared in KZine, 2015.
88	"We Are Brady" first appeared in Daily Flash in 2011. Reprinted in Fifty Flashes, 2017.
91	"C.O.D.D." first appeared in The Talespinner, 1996. Reprinted by Tigershark, 2016.
97	"Burning Away The Tears Burning Away the Years" first appeared in The Drabbler Issue #1, 2004.
98	"Debbie Does Deuce" first appeared in Jackhammer E-Zine, 1998. Reprinted in The Nth Degree Online, 2003; Honorable Mention in Tales From The Moonlit Path Contest, 2008.
102	"The Sweetest Good-Bye" first appeared in Vermont Ink, 1998.
106	"Badgers For Christmas" first appeared in Blue Gonk II, 2018. Reprinted in Sirens Call, 2018 and Scary Snippets, 2019.
111	"Bagging It" first appeared in Blue Murder E-Zine, 1999.
115	"Do The Right Thing" first appeared in Bohemia, 2014.
124	"Not A Remote Chance" first appeared in the Futures Mysterious Fiction Anthology, 2004. Reprinted in Strange Mysteries 4, 2012.
130	"Gingersnap Christmas" first appeared in Country Gazette, 1996. Reprinted in Dogwood Tales, 1997 and Darke County Magazine, 2004.
134	"Not The Remotest Hope For Adam And Eve" first appeared in The Drabbler Issue #3, 2005.
135	"To The Farm" first appeared in Blue Murder E-Zine, 1998. Nominated for a Derringer Award in 1999. Reprinted in The Jersey Ghouls, 1999, The Best Of Blue Murder, 2003, and Maelstrom, 2019. Won first place in the Spinetinglers contest in 2012.
140	"A Small Misunderstanding" first appeared in The Drabbler Special Edition 2. Reprinted in Drabble Dark, 2018.

Personal Acknowledgements

I'd like to thank everyone who helped me write and produce the stories in this book including: the Writers of the Night (Nancy Bowker, Beverly Haaf and the late Anna Hagman), Rhyss DeCassilene for her editing skills and much appreciated opinions, my sister Roslyn who had to listen to me talk about the stories all the time, my friend Marie for being the first to read my early stories back when they were handwritten, my two children, Kat and Stephen, who inspired many of the stories through their actions while growing up and who helped with their suggestions when I'd write myself into a corner, and of course, my husband, Tom, who has to stop whatever he's doing to help me whenever my computer doesn't listen to me and who graciously accepts living life with a writer.

About the Author

Writing under the name Diane Arrelle, I have had over 350 short stories published as well as three books including my dark collection of horror stories, *Seasons on The Dark Side* and this new improved version of *Just A Drop In The Cup*.

I live on the edge of the Pine Barrens (home of the Jersey Devil) in Southern New Jersey with my sane husband, and my insane cat. I am proud to be one of the founding

Diane Arrelle

members and the second president of the Garden State Horror Writers. I was also the past president of the Philadelphia Writers' Conference as well as currently on the PWC board of directors.

I began writing stories in college while taking the four-hour once-a-week class, The Geography of Southeast Asia, which I needed for my teaching certification in social studies. It was a really long class that begged to let my imagination roam. Growing up extremely rural, I naturally turned to writing speculative stories of aliens, UFO's, unicorns, fairies and of course all sorts of monsters.

To support my writing habit over the decades, I have held a wide variety of jobs including Teacher, School Bus Driver, Waitress, Salesclerk, Mystery Shopper, Holiday Gift Wrapper, Newspaper Correspondent, Tutor, Freelance Writer, Author, Columnist, Senior Citizen Center Director and that person who stood in a mall burning vanilla tinged milk and cooking tasteless crepes to sell nonstick pots and pans.

Since I have retired from all those jobs except Author, I can now add Copy-Editor, Anthology Editor and Publisher to the list.

You can visit me at https://www.arrellewrites.com
and
https://www.jerseypinesink.com

Upcoming books from Jersey Pines Ink
https://www.jerseypinesink.com/

See what JPI has to offer.

Death Spins an Indigo Web,
a Mystery and Romance novel by Ivy C. Leigh

The Chanting, a Supernatural/Romance Novel
by Beverly T. Haaf

WhoDunit,
An anthology of 34 Mysteries edited by Dina A. Leacock

Ready for your reading pleasure
available now.

Series: ***JumpRope Chronicles*** by Ivy C. Leigh

Death Behind the Lilacs

Death Counts the Golden Coins

E-Book ***Jump Into***

Seasons on the Dark Side, a Horror Short Story Collection
by Diane Arrelle

***Crypt Gnats, an Anthology of Horror Stories You've been Itching
to Read***, edited by Dina A. Leacock

JERSEY PINES INK

JPI

We Are Romance.
and Supernatural Mysteries

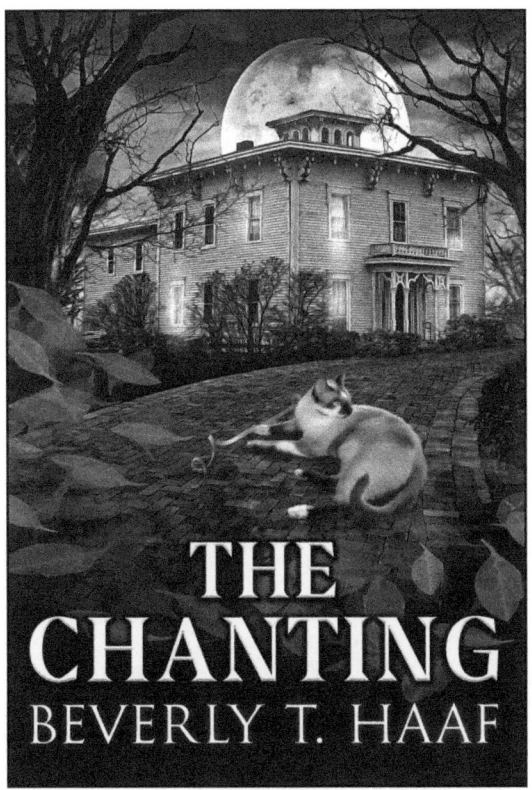

A woman, a child, and a man . . .
Will the spell of the mysterious yellow house
draw them together or tear them apart?

JERSEY PINES INK

https://www.jerseypinesink.com

JPI

We Are Mysteries

An anthology of WhoDunits and HowDunits by 34 mystery writers.

JERSEY PINES INK

https://www.jerseypinesink.com

JPI

We Are a Colorful Mystery and Romance Series

The Newest book in the JumpRope Chronical series.

JERSEY PINES INK

https://www.jerseypinesink.com

Milton Keynes UK
Ingram Content Group UK Ltd.
UKHW051030030124
435356UK00010B/204